The Spirit Line

Bipin Parekh

Contents

Chapter 1: The Funeral Parlor's Son

I hate the way the gravel crunches beneath my sneakers. It's too loud, too harsh, like the sound of my own thoughts being ground into dust. It follows me across the schoolyard, each step an echo that fills the empty spaces between the mockery. I keep my head down, eyes fixed on the path ahead, praying the world won't notice me. But it does. Always does.

The laughter starts low, a murmur that rises with every footstep. "Here comes the Grim Reaper!" The words bite into the air like a snake, sharp and venomous. I don't look up, but I feel the eyes. The boys, Keyur among them, their faces twisted in that cruel, familiar grin. They don't understand. None of them do. They don't see how their words settle deep inside me, curling into my chest, knotting into something heavy.

I kick at the gravel again, harder this time, sending a cascade of tiny stones scattering in all directions. My mind's elsewhere, somewhere far from here. Somewhere I can't escape, but where at least the weight of their words doesn't crush me. The teasing's always the same, always a joke. Always about my dad. Always about the funeral parlour. They had a nickname for my dad. They called him Doctor Death.

I could feel their eyes on me, but I didn't want to meet them. Not today. Not when the air feels thick with something else, something heavier than the usual mockery. I walk faster, but my feet feel slow, like they're dragging me into a place I don't want to be. It's always the same, like I'm stuck in a loop of their voices, the cruel laughter, the whispers behind my back. I should be used to it by now.

But the words sting.

I catch a glimpse of Keyur standing there with his hands shoved in his pockets, his face painted with the look he gives when he knows I'm listening. Keyur is my best friend. He looks embarrassed that people in his school could be so nasty. My school was mainly white English kids. Radlett was a small town and there weren't many Asian or Black kids there. The school was quite racist. Keyur says, "Let's go to the playground and kick the football around." While we are walking to the playground, Keyur says light-heartedly, "Come on Grim Reaper, let's join someone's football match." I start laughing loudly.

I glance up, just for a second, enough to see them still laughing, their voices rising again, louder, echoing like ghosts in the distance. And then it hits me, it's not just their laughter. It's me. This feeling of being torn apart inside, like the weight of every joke is a thousand bricks piled on top of me. I don't know how to escape it.

So, I walk faster. But the gravel keeps crunching, and the laughter follows. Always following.

The smell of antiseptic lingers in the air, mixing with the faint scent of stale incense. It's a smell that's become a part of me now, like an old coat that doesn't ever quite lose its weight. The door creaks as I step inside the funeral parlour. A sigh slips from my lips, soft but heavy, like I'm carrying a weight that no one else can see. I don't want to be here. But here I am, always.

The room is dim, the flickering overhead lights casting a sickly yellow glow on everything. The walls are lined with faded portraits of strangers, their eyes staring back at me, hollow and lifeless. They're watching. Always watching. I set my backpack down with a dull thud, and the quiet of the place swallows me whole. My dad, Prakash, is somewhere in the back room, his voice a low murmur that I can't quite make out. He's talking to someone. It's a tone I've grown accustomed to, calm, professional, detached. It's never for me.

I move to the waiting room, where the chairs are scattered haphazardly, like abandoned thoughts. A couple of magazines lie on the table, one slightly askew, the glossy covers barely catching the light. I pick them up slowly, each one feeling heavier than the last. A sports magazine, a gossip rag, something about celebrities. They're distractions. Nothing more. I stack them in a neat pile, my fingers lingering on the edges of the pages. I want to close my eyes, to disappear for just a second. But there's no time. There's never any time.

The bell above the door chimes. It's faint, almost delicate, but to me, it rings like an alarm. A new body. It's here. I can feel it, the chill in the air shifting just slightly. The weight of it presses in, heavy and suffocating. I've grown numb to it, this endless parade of arrivals, but that doesn't mean I'm used to it. Not really. The air seems to freeze as I stand there, unsure for just a moment. What does it mean? What does it matter? They come. They go.

I glance toward the back room, where my father stands, his silhouette cast against the dim light. The faint murmur of his voice continues, but I know what comes next. It always does. My job. His job. Our job. The same routine, the same sorrow hanging thick in the air. The thought makes my chest tighten, a knot that refuses to loosen. I don't want to do this. But I will. I always do.

The door creaked open with that familiar groan, like the slow stretch of an old man's bones, and I knew, without looking, that another body had arrived. My father, Prakash, moved in like a shadow, his face unreadable, his steps measured and deliberate. The room, already heavy with the air of death, thickened just a little more as he nodded toward me, his eyes flicking briefly to mine before settling on the body that had been wheeled in.

"Time to check the pockets," he said, his voice flat, a note of finality to it that sent a cold shiver down my spine.

I winced, just for a second, though I knew better than to show it. But something inside me twisted, a knot forming in my stomach. It was the ritual, the part of the job that always felt too real, too close. I followed my father's movements closely, the dull scrape of his shoes against the polished floor marking the rhythm of this routine I couldn't escape. He worked with the body as though it was just another object, another thing to be processed. His fingers moved with practiced precision, turning the clothes, feeling the fabric, searching for something, anything, that could be tucked away.

Each time the body arrives, it's the same. The stillness. The silence that fills the room after the death. As if all the warmth had been drained out of it, leaving nothing but a hollow shell behind. I never got used to it, not really. I couldn't.

Prakash's hands moved quickly pulling out the usual things: a worn wallet, a watch with the glass cracked, a mobile phone which will never hear his owner's voice in the phone ever again, a few stray coins that had somehow clung to life despite the cold.

"Put these in the safe," he muttered, still not sparing me more than a cursory glance.

I nodded, a tight, mechanical movement, as I walked toward the safe. Each step felt heavier than the last. I opened the door and slid the items inside, the cold metal biting at my fingertips. As I closed the door, a sharp buzz from my pocket caught me off guard. My phone. I'd forgotten about it, and now the faint buzz seemed to echo through the still room like a far-off warning.

I pulled it out, half-heartedly glancing at the screen before setting it aside. The weight of the phone, like everything else here, seemed inconsequential, a distraction, a flicker of life in a place where nothing was truly alive anymore. I pushed the thought away. Jayesh took his phone out of his pocket and saw a message from Keyur: 'Do you want to play the PlayStation after dinner? I can come to your house.' Keyur and Jayesh played football on the PlayStation all the time. It was their favourite game. There were things to be done. I had chores. I always had chores.

The place smelled of stale incense and antiseptic, the scent clinging to my clothes as I went out of the funeral parlour and went to the side entrance to our flat above the funeral parlour.

Jayesh went to the kitchen to see his mum. Jayesh's mum was a very loving person. When Jayesh went to the kitchen, his mum gave him a great big smile and a hug. Jayesh felt so comforted.

"How was your day today at school?"

"Fine," Jayesh said.

"Jayesh, I am starving. I've made your favourite today, aloo gobi and paratha. Set the table." Mina calls to Shivani, Jayesh's 8-year-old sister.

The phone in Jayesh's pocket buzzed suddenly. He took the phone out of his pocket and glanced at it. It wasn't his phone.

"Damn," Jayesh said to himself. He had put the dead guy's phone in his pocket by mistake instead of putting it in the safe. He picked up the phone and said, "Hello? Hello?" but there was only a crackling sound.

Jayesh goes to his room after dinner, satisfied and happy, sits at his desk and does his homework. He hears a tap at his door, it's Keyur, his friend. 'Hi Jayesh, I am going to completely beat you today at FIFA.' They pick their teams: Jayesh picks his favourite team, Tottenham, and Keyur picks his favourite team, Arsenal. Keyur looks at the phone on Jayesh's desk and asks, 'Whose phone is this?' Jayesh tells him how he forgot to put it in the safe. Jayesh and Keyur have a few matches on the PlayStation. Prakash, Jayesh's dad, knocks on Jayesh's door and says, 'Come on, boys, time to wrap it up. Keyur, you need to go home. You both have school in the morning.'

Jayesh goes to sleep but is woken up by the buzz of the mobile phone. He ignores it and goes back to sleep. Jayesh's alarm clock goes off. Jayesh looks out of the window and sees the morning light creeping through the gaps of his curtains. He checks the clock to see what time it is and gets out of bed. He goes to the bathroom then comes back to his bedroom. Jayesh puts his school uniform on. Just then the phone rings again. He answers the phone. At first there was nothing but static. Jayesh thought it was bad connection, maybe a prank. But then a voice broke through, faint and trembling. Help me, it said.

"Who is this?" Jayesh asked.

"My name is Rumesh, Jayesh. I need your help."

"Is this some sort of joke? Who is this really?"

"I am RUMESH. Please believe me. I am dead, and I am in your funeral parlour."

Jayesh froze. His heart hammered in his chest, loud and thudding. The hairs on the back of his neck stood up. His hands shook, the phone almost slipping from his grip. His mind screamed to hang up, to ignore it, but he couldn't. Something about that voice, it wasn't just a voice. It was something else, something too real, too urgent.

"Who is this?" Jayesh croaked, his voice barely above a whisper, afraid to speak too loudly, afraid the voice would vanish if he did.

"I'm Rumesh," the voice responded, trembling. "I... need help."

"Rumesh, how can I help you?" Rumesh starts to tell Jayesh why his soul is not at peace.

"I was with my daughter Seema at the swimming pool. We were having a good time. Seema is only 8 years old. Seema was playing with her toys at the side of the pool. She had a small inflatable frog. I kicked it in the pool just to have a bit of fun with Seema. Seema thought she dropped the toy in the pool. She said, 'Daddy, my toy, look, it's in the pool.' I said to her as a joke, 'Don't worry, here comes Super Dad.' I jumped in, but as I was jumping in, I had a massive heart attack and hit my head on the side of the pool. People thought I was just messing around. When I was floating face down in the water, the lifeguard jumped in to save me. But it was too late. The massive heart attack killed me while I was jumping in. My daughter Seema is absolutely distraught. She thinks she has killed her dad."

Jayesh can't believe he is talking to a ghost.

Jayesh said, "Are you a ghost?"

Rumesh jokingly said, "No, I am not a ghost. I am a spirit, a disturbed spirit."

Jayesh said, "Rumesh, I am only 13 years old. I need to speak to my mum and dad first."

Jayesh blinked, his pulse pounding. Rumesh? The name echoed in his head, but he couldn't place it. It didn't make sense. "What happened?" Jayesh asked, his voice shaking now.

Jayesh tells Rumesh, "Can you please repeat this same story to my parents?"

Rumesh said, "I don't think your parents or anyone else will be able to hear me because I think you need a gift to listen to spirits from the other side."

"Okay, but I still need to speak to my parents."

Rumesh says, "Okay, sure."

Jayesh goes downstairs to the living room, and his mum Mina, dad Prakash, and sister Shivani are at the dinner table waiting for him.

His dad says, "Come in Jayesh, what were you doing in your room? You are going to be late for school."

Mina says, "Come on Jayesh, have your breakfast."

Mina looks at Jayesh and asks, "What's the matter, Jayesh?" She always knew if there was anything on his mind.

"Mum, Dad, I got something to tell you. You are both going to think I am mad, but I need to tell you."

Jayesh starts to tell them what happened, how he forgot to put Rumesh's phone in the safe and left it in his pocket, how the phone buzzed yesterday and he picked it up and there was only static, and how it buzzed again in the morning. Then Jayesh told them that in the morning when it buzzed again, a voice came through to him. He said his name was Rumesh and told him why he needed his help.

Jayesh told them what Rumesh said, why he needed his help. He told them about Seema and the heart attack, and how Seema was blaming herself. She thought because she dropped the toy in the water and told her dad to go in the swimming pool to get it, her dad hit his head in the pool and died.

Prakash looked absolutely stunned. Mina had a look of amazement on her face, and Shivani burst out laughing.

"Please don't laugh," Mina said.

Mina said to Prakash, "Are you taking drugs in your room or what? Or is it these silly games you are playing on the PlayStation that have got to your head?"

Mina asked Prakash, "What is the name of the body in the funeral parlour?"

Prakash said with bewilderment, "Rumesh. How would Jayesh know his name?"

"Prakash, come on. Mina, you don't really think Jayesh is speaking to spirits, do you?"

Mina looks at Prakash and Jayesh and says, "Prakash, you know this gift runs in my family."

"What?" said Jayesh surprisingly.

"Yes Jayesh, your grandmother has the gift as well, and your auntie Riya has the gift as well, and your great-grandmother too."

Prakash is looking at Mina in amazement.

"Okay look Jayesh, you need to get to school or you will be late."

In front of Jayesh, Keyur arrived walking towards him with that lopsided grin of his, the one that made him look like he was always in on some joke the rest of them weren't. But when he saw Jayesh's face, his smile faded just for a second. Jayesh didn't say anything, didn't need to. He knew Keyur could tell. Keyur always knew when something was wrong.

"I know this sounds crazy," Jayesh started, his voice tight trying to shake the unease that curled around his chest like smoke, "but I think a man named Rumesh who is in my father's funeral parlour is trying to contact me. His daughter thinks he drowned trying to get her toy out of the swimming pool. She thinks it's her fault her father died."

Keyur raised an eyebrow, his expression shifting from confusion to disbelief.

"Wait, you're saying a ghost called you? Well yes," Jayesh said. "OK but don't let anyone at school hear you say you can speak to ghosts or they will make up more nicknames for you," said Keyur with a surprised look on his face.

After school, when Jayesh gets home, his mum and dad are waiting for him in the living room.

"Come Jayesh, sit down next to me," his mum says.

Jayesh sits down and his dad looks at him and says, "Okay Jayesh, what does Rumesh's spirit want you to do?"

Jayesh says, "I need to speak to him to ask him what he wants me to do."

Jayesh gets Rumesh's phone and switches it on. They have to wait until he calls him.

Jayesh tells his parents. They all wait nervously looking at the phone. Mina, Jayesh's mum, takes her own phone out of her pocket and calls her mother Manorama in India.

"Jayesh, your grandmother wants to speak to you."

"Hello, Dadi Ma," Jayesh says.

Manorama says, "How are you, my sweetheart?"

"I am well," says Jayesh.

Manorama says, "Listen son, you have a fantastic gift son. There is nothing to be frightened of. You are helping a lost spirit and helping a family with their grief."

Just then Rumesh's phone rings. Everyone in the room acts like they have been hit by a bolt of lightning.

Jayesh answers the phone,

"Hello? Hello?"

Rumesh's voice comes out of the phone with a sigh of relief.

"Hello Jayesh, thank you for answering my phone. How can I help you?"

Rumesh says, "Listen Jayesh, my daughter is so hurt and depressed. You need to go and see my wife and tell them they need to tell the hospital to do an autopsy on my body so they will know the truth. Once they do the autopsy, they will know how I died of a massive heart attack and my daughter will not think I died because of her. Please Jayesh, I need your help. This could save my daughter from a lifetime of misery."

Jayesh tells Rumesh, "I need to relay this message to my parents."

"Sure," says Rumesh.

Jayesh tells his parents what Rumesh has just said.

Jayesh's dad says, "Ask him for something only he would know so when we go there, his wife would believe you."

Jayesh tells Rumesh, "I am just a 13-year-old kid. If I go to your house without any proof, they will throw me out of your house."

Rumesh says, "Okay, you're right. My wife's name is Nalini and my daughter's name is Seema. Tell my wife there is a safe in my wardrobe floor. It's concealed beneath a secret panel. In the safe, there are four diamond rings, five thousand pounds in cash, and paperwork for an apartment in Goa, a surprise gift for the family. Please tell them this, then they will believe you."

Prakash says, "We need to go quickly so this poor little girl and Rumesh's wife knows the truth."

"Can I take Keyur as well?"

"No," said Prakash, "he will think you are mad."

"I have told him what happened. He is my best friend. Let Jayesh take Keyur. He will be good support for him."

"Okay, come, let's go," said Prakash.

Jayesh calls Keyur and tells him, "We are going to Rumesh's house. Do you want to come?"

"Try to stop me," Keyur says enthusiastically.

They pick up Keyur on the way to Rumesh's house.

Rumesh lives in Stanmore in Harrow.

In the car, Keyur stayed quiet on the journey to Stanmore, doing that thing with his mouth where he was deep in thought, clearly overloaded in his brain. After a minute he let out a sigh suggesting that for whatever reason he was going to give up on trying to make his mind work.

"Jayesh, you're really sure about this?"

As they drove up to Rumesh's house, Jayesh's stomach started to churn and twist like he was sitting on a frightening roller coaster. Rumesh's house was beautiful with a long driveway. As they got to the top of the driveway, Keyur said in a slight voice, "Here we go."

They got out of the car and Jayesh's dad said, "Are you okay son? Don't worry, I am here beside you." The words gave Jayesh strength within.

Prakash rang the doorbell. The door opened slowly, creaking. The world outside was slipping away momentarily.

Nalini stood at the doorway with a look of confusion and grief. Shadows were cast across her face while the light from within the house spilled outside, but her features were explaining her exhaustion. Jayesh could tell that her dark and heavy eyes held some unexplainable sadness. She was a woman suffocated by thick sorrow which had restrained her body like skin.

"Hello, how can I help you?" said Nalini. She was a tall slim lady; she looked as if she was crying.

Prakash said, "My name is Prakash. We are handling your late husband Rumesh's funeral."

"Okay, is everything okay?" asked Nalini.

"Yes, I wonder if I can have a chat with you."

"Sure, please come in."

They go into Rumesh's house. It's a very big house with bright coloured walls and pictures of Hindu gods on the wall and a big family photo in the hallway.

In the large living room, they see Seema sitting on the sofa playing a game on a phone. This is my daughter Seema. She has a withdrawn look about her. You can see both mother and daughter have been crying. Seema says, "Hello uncle," to Prakash and "Hello," to Keyur and Jayesh.

They sit down.

Jayesh's dad says, "Nalini Bhen, please can we have a word in private?"

Nalini looks surprised, "Sure, okay, no problem."

Let's go in the kitchen.

They go in the kitchen and sit around the dining table.

"How can I help you, Prakash Bhai?"

Jayesh's dad says, "Nalini Bhen, there is no easy way to say this so please let me just say what I have come here to tell you."

Prakash starts from the beginning. He starts with how Jayesh had Rumesh's phone and how it rang and how Jayesh spoke to Rumesh, and what he told Jayesh and he told her about how this gift was passed down to Jayesh from generations of Mina's side of the family. He explains what Rumesh said about how he died and it was not Seema's fault.

"You don't know anything about my husband's death, so how could you?" she queried.

Prakash, a soft tone for a question that was hard spoken in a sharp tone revealing bits of air's tension.

Nalini looked flabbergasted. "What proof do you have? How can I believe a child?"

Following her words, Jayesh felt a sharpness grip his throat, momentarily imprisoning him. His mouth wanted to express how he don't know the reason and the situation is way too complicated for him, but explaining was off the table now, and he was forced to follow even if he lacked deep comprehension. Jayesh didn't understand at the moment, but one thing he certainly knew without overthinking, this is how it is. Well, this is how Jayesh came to believe it is.

"There's a safe in the wardrobe floor," the words felt certain and way too confident for Jayesh's own liking. Jayesh knew better than to be so convinced, not until this moment at least. A long-buried instinct had awoken.

"It's concealed beneath a panel," said Jayesh.

Nalini looked at Jayesh as she was going to pounce on him. She was looking at Jayesh differently now. Her brows were knitted in thought, and her lips were fused in that skeptical pout parents wear when they think their child is saying an elaborate yarn trying to get away from some mischief they have done. But then, as if something inside Jayesh had unlocked, the floodgates of his mouth opened.

"There are four diamond rings, five thousand pounds in cash, and paperwork for an apartment in Goa, a surprise gift for the family."

Nalini looked at Jayesh completely differently when Jayesh revealed the secret of what was in the safe. You can see it in her face; she started to believe. Nalini walked up to Jayesh. She had a tear in her eye. She held his hand and started to cry.

"Thank you for coming to see me. I know it must have been hard for a young boy, but Jayesh, can I please speak to him?"

Jayesh said, "You won't be able to communicate with him; only I can speak to him."

Nalini fell to her knees and touched Jayesh's feet and said sobbing, "Please Jayesh, please just try."

Jayesh said, "Auntie, I am so sorry you won't be able to hear him."

Prakash interrupted, "Nalini Bhen, please get up. Not even we can hear anything on the phone; we can only hear static."

"I am sorry Jayesh to put you in this position."

"That's okay Auntie."

Nalini asks, "What else did Rumesh say?"

"That's all. He wants you to tell the hospital to take his body and do an autopsy so they can reveal he had a massive heart attack. He is so worried about Seema. He knows she thinks it's her fault. He wants her to know it wasn't her fault. It had nothing to do with her. You need to get this autopsy done Auntie, please."

At that moment Seema walked into the kitchen. She went up to her mum and hugged her. They both burst out crying.

"I heard everything mum."

Nalini hugged her tighter.

Nalini said, "I will get the autopsy done ASAP."

Nalini tells Prakash and Jayesh, "Thank you so much for coming. I will get the autopsy done in the morning." She said goodbye to Prakash and gave a hug to Jayesh and Keyur.

In the car on the way home, Prakash looked at Jayesh in the mirror and said, "Jayesh, I am so proud of you. Well done and thank you for coming with us. Keyur, for giving your support to Jayesh."

"No problem uncle," said Keyur, "Jayesh is my best friend."

They drop off Keyur at home and go home.

When they get home, Prakash tells Mina everything. Mina listens and has a great big smile on her face and gives Jayesh a kiss on the cheek.

"Well done my love."

The next day the hospital calls Prakash and says, "Nalini wants an autopsy done of the body of her husband Rumesh. We are coming to collect the body."

An hour later the ambulance arrives and wheels Rumesh's body out.

Jayesh can imagine Rumesh is looking down at him and saying, "Well done Jayesh."

When the body is wheeled past Jayesh, just for a moment he could imagine Rumesh putting his hands out of the white cloth that covered him and giving Jayesh a big thumbs up. It brought a small smile to Jayesh's face.

Prakash asked the doctor who was sitting in the ambulance, "When will the autopsy be done?"

The doctor said, "As soon as we get to the hospital. Because Nalini is paying for the autopsy, it will be done straight away. We will call Nalini to come to the hospital in 3 hours."

When the ambulance went, Jayesh asks his dad, "Can we go to the hospital as well to give them our support?"

Prakash looks at Jayesh and says, "Sure, let me give Nalini Bhen a call."

"Please can I come as well?" Mina says.

"Okay, let me give her a call."

Prakash calls Nalini. She was delighted that they offered to come to the hospital and would love their support.

In the sterile hospital air, the antiseptic tang filled the air, sharp and cold like the echo of a past Jayesh couldn't shake. There was an acute jingle of fluorescent lights that flickered a clinical quote over everything, but Jayesh couldn't focus on any of it, not even an inch. Everything besides Seema held no interest to him.

She sat in the corner of the room, shoulders hitching imperceptibly as the doctor spoke to her, his words lost to Jayesh like the drone of a car engine. Seema's face was white, almost ashen, her eyes puffy and red from the tears shed for a father who was too far away.

For so long, she had pointed an accusing finger at herself, believing that her thoughtless poolside frolic had led to his demise. The guilt that crushed her with each breath she took had dealt a relentless blow. Yet, it was all over now. Even excruciating, bittersweet truth brings relief, so long as the release one is waiting for does eventually come.

"The autopsy results confirm," the doctor said, "that Mr. Rumesh died from a massive heart attack, not from drowning." The truth slices sharper than expected, and these words fell like a lead weight, filling this room with a thick, stagnant animosity.

The details were too specific, too real under Seema's fitting gaze, and in that silence. As Jayesh soaked in Seema's frozen expression, her trembling arms tightening on the abyss of collapsing. Shoulders quaking, chest heaving, the remorseless burden lifting was all too achingly clear.

And then, it happened. Seema lost it, her tears pained and echoing off the cold walls. Each and every one of her sobs cut as if it was clawing its way out of her being, and her pain brought no solace. She cried as if shedding tears would absolve all her suffering from the past.

Mina sat beside Nalini and Seema. She put her arm around Seema and said, "Your father was a fantastic man and loved you and your mum so much. His soul couldn't rest because he knew you were in pain. Even after death, he was thinking about your happiness."

Seema turned to Mina and started to cry in her arms. Mina said, "Seema, I know grief is hard, especially for a young girl, but you must try to remember the good times you had with your father. He wouldn't want to see you unhappy."

Jayesh had a lump in his throat. Seema's silence held a weight that was unbearable. The absence of sound felt unnatural at that moment. Unbearable, even.

In Jayesh's attempt to fill the void, he was left without words. Jayesh tried to cough words, but no sound would escape. There was no way for truth to roam free now, as grief never truly made its exit. It always managed to tuck itself beneath the surface and settle into the shadows like still water itself.

Nalini wiped the tears away from Seema's face and said, "Come on, let's go home and get a pizza on the way. You must be hungry, I know I am."

Seema looked at Nalini and gave her a sympathetic look and said, "Yes, I am starving." They all got up, and Prakash went up to Seema and told her, "I am here for you and you can come to my house anytime."

Mina said, "Yes, I have a daughter your age. She would love to play together with you." Nalini hugged Mina and said, "Thank you so much for everything. I am indebted to your family forever. Your son Jayesh has saved my daughter from a life of guilt and misery."

Nalini put her hand on Jayesh's shoulder and said, "How can I ever thank you?" Jayesh replied, "It's ok, Auntie, please don't say thank you."

Jayesh and Mina got in the car with Prakash. On the way home, Mina said, "You did a lot of good today, Jayesh. You have helped a family deal with grief and a lost spirit get some peace."

When Jayesh got home, he went straight to his room. Like an unwanted guest, the night dragged away time and pressed against the corners of Jayesh's room. The only sound was the ceiling fan, which made a hum while the air was still and relaxed.

Jayesh mentally drifted away while lying on his bed, the sheets constricting around him like a barrier refusing to let him escape. The phone was right beside him, its screen reflecting faintly

The light above. The device felt alive, as I often felt after my phone calls, especially the one that obliterated my life as I knew it.

Rumesh. That name was enough to make me feel strange vibrations. I pictured him, and his face was embedded in my memory, as if plastered on a grey canvas, just out of my grasp. I buried my face into the pillow, trying to escape the reality and weight of everything that happened.

Chapter 2 - "Gayatri's Ladder"

After my first supernatural experience, I couldn't contain my excitement. I felt like a superhero who had just discovered his powers - I could actually communicate with spirits! The thought made my heart race with anticipation. What other adventures awaited me? What mysteries would I uncover?

Inside my family room, dim light pressed against the walls, warming them like a comforting shadow, but the tension remained beneath the warmth. Earlier that day, I had been doing normal thirteen-year-old activities - meeting Keyur in the garden to kick the football around, struggling through my mathematics homework, and chatting with my sister Shivani about her upcoming school dance. But now, everything felt different, charged with possibility.

My father gazed at me with eyes sharp as winter frost, piercing through the air at the very idea of my desires. I made a point to keep my eagerness on the sidelines by saying: "Please, let's see if someone else contacts me if you get another dead body." However, my father quickly responded, a protection against the mysterious: "No, I don't want you to be a stranger."

The atmosphere thickened. We were caught in a mix of sandalwood incense and fresh paint from the adjoining funeral parlor: a familiar, yet oppressive atmosphere. Prakash Patel, my father, was tall and graying of hair, a funeral director fighting against the changing tides of belief and battling the age-old traditions. His voice was clipped and resolute. "These things...they're not for you. Don't have time for ghost stories. You have to focus on your studies."

I wanted to scream, to tell him, no, whenever the dead are around, there is a still strangely warm feeling, the air buzzes with presence and it's not a bit eerie at all. How could I explain what was underneath my skin, the thought in my mind, what I felt in the night when I sleep? It was like jumping into deep waters and being not sure if I will rise up for air again.

My mother's calm but insistent tone stopped the mounting frustration. "Don't call our son a stranger; he has a gift God has given him," Mina said firmly. Mina Patel is petite with a soft grace that radiates with a light that made the room somehow less confined. She is my anchor wherever I am when things are winding, she is my believer, and I could feel her support in the most comforting blanket.

Prakash's eyes turned soft aside from the firm strain of his jaw that bore hard shades of disbelief. "A gift? It's a burden, Mina. Death isn't a game," he replied, his voice heavy with concern.

I could hear the fear in my father's voice, the worry undertone of trying to protect me from mortality's weight, and fear of the depths of the unknown. "We don't want to treat it seriously because it could lead him to the dark places," Prakash continued, his protective instincts evident.

"Jayesh's heart is pure so the dark side won't go near him and besides he is helping the spirits so he is doing a good thing - he is doing God's work," Mina replied, her gentle conviction melting some of the ice around my father's heart.

The phone rang, a jarring note in all the familial chorus before he could retort. We were all startled, and when Prakash's phone was vibrating on the table, the news that came through helped fuel an already burning fire. Downstairs, a woman, a thirty-five-year-old by the name of Gayatri had fallen from a ladder and was lifeless in the parlor.

"Look, give Jayesh the phone. Please," Mina said urgently, her voice just a little bit shaky. "She may have something to say."

"You can sense the departed's loving nature, Jayesh. There might be unfinished business," Mina stepped close, her warmth a balm against Prakash's rigid stance.

I could not dare to meet my father's gaze and held my breath. Finally, he broke, with an exasperated sigh, giving up and letting out a reluctant "OK" before reaching for the phone. His hand stayed out for a moment, almost slow against no presence in the air, before putting it inside my outstretched palm.

I was so excited to get the phone in my hand, what will happen what adventure will I be having, when will the phone ring, will it ring, questions were ringing in Jayesh's ear. Jayesh's Dad looked at Jayesh and said "you look so excited that worries me I don't want you to get too lost in this gift you have." Prakash was worried this could get out of hand and Jayesh will not concentrate on his studies.

My room was a tangled refuge of nostalgia: The wallpaper peeled slightly to show just the corner of the wooden frame. Football stars posters were looming out of the chaos of clothes and gadgets, a microcosm of a teenager's conflict on mundane life and shadows dancing outside of my reach. The old ceiling fan above me creaked lightly and I wondered if the phone of Gayatri the lady dead in my father's funeral parlour would ring tonight. My excitement was rising in my stomach like the tide in the sea.

I heard Keyur sprawl on my floor, laughing heartily, no doubt just another joke about how I would never scare him, never, not after whatever it was that had nearly killed us both. "C'mon, Jay! It's just a game. If we're going to beat the record!" he said. "We need to focus!"

He hit one of the buttons, and our digital players were sent careening all over the screen.

"Right, right! But what if...what if the phone rings? Will it be easy to handle?" I offered, my voice wavering between humor and deeper concern.

Jayesh and Keyur keep playing Fifa on the PlayStation they are both in a great jovial mood. Jayesh wins the match on the PlayStation and puts Keyur in a head lock and says "who is best Keyur come on say my name" then Keyur reluctantly says "ok you are now let me go."

His eyes gleamed playfully and he chuckled. "And then we will have what's now known to be an impromptu ghost guest. That'd be a plot twist!" We had the easiest camaraderie; laughter bounced off of the worries I had. The boy who would jump to his death right in front of me, because we were like brothers and I know I can rely on him.

By midnight, the air changed, a tangible energy softly passed through the room. Heart beating louder than the sound of frantic gaming we were doing, I kept glancing at the phone. "Do you really believe she will pick up the phone?" My throat was suddenly dry, and I murmured.

His tone was serious but laced with excitement, and Keyur leaned closer towards him. "Not every day, huh, dude? My friend gets a direct line to the dead. Perhaps she has a very unhappy incident she has to share with you and she needs you to put things right for her. Whatever it is you will be helping a lost soul. When people find out at school you will be the coolest kid in school, Keyur please you can't tell anyone people you must promise me."

With a smile that I managed, the bubbling anticipation felt unsettling. Keyur said don't worry I won't tell anyone what do you think I can tell them. They will think we are both mad, we are already the most unpopular kids in our year. We both waited with bated breath glancing at the phone now and again.

Then it happened. They interrupted, the ringing of the phone and entered a harsh sound echoing through the silence that has been enveloping all of us. I could only grin and look at Keyur, who smiled and gave me a look to indicate 'go on'. "Come on, pick it up," he enticed, Keyur felt the same excitement as I did.

I took a deep breath holding the receiver in my hands it was a connection to the outside world I had only engaged. The weight of it feels in my hand as I said yes and sadness grew, hidden behind layers, and uncontrollable thoughts may lurk. "Hello?"

A crackle penetrated through the air and then a whispered voice, or a growl which resembled the sound of leaves in the night. "Hello, can you hear me?"

"Yes I can," I replied almost whispering to her. The walls of the room closed in on me and I felt like they had their own heartbeat.

This resonating voice proceeded to pull me in deeper into the abyss. "My name is Gayatri. I'm in the morgue downstairs. Please, can you help me?"

This made me feel the cold sweat run down my spine and I could visibly feel the density of her words in the chest. My throat was parched and I swallowed nervously before I was able to choke out, "Of course, go ahead and tell me what is wrong."

And that is when the threads of my everyday life began to come loose at the seams and become the fabric of a world where I am linked to the mysterious, unknown, and an unstoppable force of the Other Side.

Gayatri's Story

Gayatri's voice on the other end of the phone was shy like a spider web yet she entrapped me with her voice. I looked at Keyur sitting across the room; he grew closer, looked like a mixture of excitement and fear in his eyes. The light was from the television still showing the stopped football match throwing the shadows on the wall, motion as it were alive but propelled by the spirit. Only I could hear Gayatri's voice - that was my gift. If I had put the phone on speaker, no sound would have come out for anyone else to hear.

"Everyone thinks I fell off the ladder," she began, her voice measured and clinical despite the weight of what she was revealing. "But I didn't. The wind blew leaves into the gutter on my roof, and I had to go up to clear them out. That's when Jason saw his opportunity."

The accident that occurred at this spot made many people think that she slid off a ladder, although this was not the case at all. She began to tell me about Jason Thomas, her neighbor - a man who had been a long-time shadow in her life.

"I have a neighbor who has been following me. He thinks I like him," she spoke faster as if she did not want the wind to take her words away from her mouth. "I left my husband to go our separate ways because he was an alcoholic and used to beat me up."

It was a sad narrative of a woman whose life was an epitome of betrayal, fear, and desperation that was woven into a web. Jason Thomas, the neighbor, was a friend of her ex-husband's. It had begun with crude text messages, excuses, attempts to get close to her sexually when his wife was not around. Every revelation was a stone flung into the water of my developing mind; the right as well as the wrong bewildered me about the reality of the adult world.

"I got the house when we divorced. But Jason came by, asking if I was okay, offering help," she continued, her voice taking on a darker tone. "Then it was WhatsApp messages, inappropriate ones. He blamed being drunk, and he apologized. But it got worse."

She told me about the night when Jason's wife Sarah went to visit her mother in Scotland. "One evening, I heard Jason knock on my door. He'd been drinking. He sat on my sofa and cried, crying about his life." I felt a horrifying blend of pity and panic, pity for this woman's vulnerability and the unfolding tragedy.

"He told me he was falling in love with me. I told him no with stark clarity. But he didn't understand it. He tried to force himself upon me; he tried to kiss me. I pushed him away."

Her voice shook as she recounted the escalation. "Still, he kept sending WhatsApps. I had threatened to tell his wife and the police. He said he'd stop. But one day, I was on the ladder. He saw me come out and pulled away the ladder."

The temperature seemed to drop and the atmosphere in the room drew in rapidly when she said that. Keyur's face had turned pale and the controller had fallen from his hands by this time. "Jay," he said in a low tone, "this is very serious business."

"I fell and hit my head. I smashed my head on the ground," she continued, her voice teetering as if she were living that moment again. "Then he finished what he started. He killed me."

I pictured her in my head like she was standing in front of me, even though I could only hear her voice through the phone. It was a burden of trust that lay on my shoulders with the power of Gayatri's trust when I hadn't desired it when I asked for this gift. "What do you want us to do?" I asked her, taking a deep breath before speaking.

"Please, go to my brother," she negotiated with desperate urgency. "Tell Umesh to go to the police to retrieve the deleted WhatsApps and check the deleted CCTV footage. Jason went into my house to delete everything, but there should still be traces that can be recovered."

"Me and Keyur are children," I said, settling back to reality from the magical scene. "Your brother won't believe us."

"His name is Umesh. We lived in Wembley, North West London," she went on, not to be discouraged. Then, with a rush of remembrance, came a keepsake, personal and concrete. She told me about when she and her brother and cousin Priya buried a time capsule in a park in Wembley when they were children.

"We lived in Wembley when we were children, me, Umesh, and our cousin Priya. We buried a time capsule to dig up when we're 60," she said, her memories lighting up with an urgency that reminded me of the innocence we once had. "I put in a Barbie doll and two

books, Famous Five and James and the Giant Peach.
Umesh put his action man toy and a Roy of the Rovers
magazine. Priya added her Barbie and her all-clear
cancer hospital results."

"How old were you?" Caught up in her web of nostalgia
and grief, I whispered over the line.

"Me and Priya were 9," she replied. "Umesh was 11."

I suddenly realized the cold emptiness, the stillness of
the voice, the almost detached manner in which she had
spoken were the hallmarks of genuine despair. The
phone's display went dim and the only sound remaining
was silence.

After the call ended, I immediately turned to Keyur and
told him everything about my conversation with
Gayatri. His eyes widened with each detail I shared - the
stalking neighbor, the deliberate murder disguised as an
accident, the deleted evidence. Keyur sat in stunned
silence, his face growing paler as the full horror of what
we had learned sank in.

"Jay, this is incredible," Keyur whispered, his voice
shaking. "She was actually murdered. That man Jason
Thomas killed her and made it look like an accident. We
have to do something - we're the only ones who know
the truth."

"We need to tell someone," Keyur said at last, his voice
clear despite the quiver in his palm. "It's not just ghost
stories anymore. This is murder."

I simply nodded, comprehendingly. "Tomorrow," I
decided. "Let's postpone this conversation until
morning; we need to process everything we've learned."

That night, sleep evaded me. Sometimes, I couldn't
sleep, the ceiling and the door were covered with
shadows, and I could only hear Gayatri's voice in my
head. It was one thing to have faith and to empower the
notion of believing in spirits and the ability for the dead
to communicate with their loved ones. But to be handed
the task to become a justice seeker, to become a voice
for a lady who could not speak for herself; this was
something that I had not expected.

Finding Umesh

The next morning shone bright, though gray clouds
overhead painted the world in muted tones as I walked
with Keyur, our footfalls breaking the silence like
whispers of secrets upon pavement. With Gayatri's
message heavy on our minds and horror thrumming
through our hearts, every step taken towards Umesh's
flat in Harrow had a solemn weight.

As we walked, I noticed how Keyur's brow furrowed in
concentration, as did mine. The uneasy silence between
us was a burden, something heavy and palpable

compared to the muted clamor of the city around us. What if he didn't believe us? What if he would never see the truth?

As we came to Umesh's fairly basic flat, the weight of our mission seemed to increase further. A gray, oppressive structure stood before us, the paint faded and peeling, mirroring the devastation of the past week. The door seemed unwelcoming. Keyur and I exchanged a glance: this was it.

I raised my trembling fist and knocked. The sound echoed through the tight space, amplifying our anxious silence as we waited. Minutes felt like hours before the door creaked open, and I saw Umesh standing there, arms crossed tightly across his chest. Skepticism tinged his features as he scrutinized us through the narrow opening.

"Who are you?" Umesh's tone was weary, almost afraid of what he might hear.

I stammered over my words as my heart thrummed in my ears. "We're friends of Gayatri," I said. "We have something important to share." His eyes narrowed, making my stomach sink.

"Friends? What kind of friends?" There was an edge to his skepticism that couldn't be missed, a hint of distrust.

"Her voice..." I barely could keep my words steady, but pressed on: "She reached out to us. We heard what happened. She recorded a message before..." The implications fell over me like a shroud. "She needs your help."

When I said Gayatri's name, I caught a glimmer in Umesh's eyes, something hidden deep under pain and disbelief. "But why would I trust you?" he shot back, arms still folded.

Keyur took over, his voice calm despite his obvious nervousness. "We have evidence. She talked about a time capsule. You shared it as children. If you remember..."

The tension suspended between us seemed electric as Umesh processed the information. Memories came rushing back, and I could see the walls closing in on him.

"What are you talking about?" Despite himself, his interest was piqued and he leaned closer.

With desperation in my words, I pressed on. "She spoke about burying a time capsule together in Wembley, the things you each put inside."

Suddenly, as if struck by lightning, something changed inside Umesh. Disbelief became anguish, and his arms fell to his sides. "You really knew about that?" His voice was raw, trembling.

"The doll, the books... It's all there," I said, seeing comprehension dawn on him. "What she needs is for you to go to the police."

That broke him. His composure shattered as his memories emerged from their vaults. He turned and raced to the phone on the nearby table. "I need to call them! I need to..." His hands fumbled in frantic urgency as he attempted to dial, his heart racing with such urgency.

Keyur and I exchanged anxious glances as Umesh made the call, his voice pleading and desperate. I felt my pulse quicken as the reality of what was before us edged into tangible clarity.

Justice for Gayatri

Within hours, the police response began to unfurl. Officers arrived at Gayatri's home, their investigation systematic and thorough. I was anxious, waiting for their return with the burden of proof. What could they uncover? Would her recorded pleas be heard from beyond the grave?

The scene around us escalated. I found myself outside under the flickering light of a streetlamp, surrounded by a group of hushed onlookers. Gayatri's home now seemed to hold the raw truth as officers methodically collected evidence - including a hard drive containing her final messages that Jason had failed to completely delete.

In a jarring moment that felt like justice finally arriving, Jason Thomas was led away from an adjacent house, handcuffed and disheveled, disbelief etched onto his face. Cameras flashed all around us, cataloging this moment of reckoning. There were murmurs from the crowd, shadows of judgment in their voices.

Gayatri's spirit weighed on me in the air, intermingling with my thoughts. The taste was bitter and sweet - victory was hard-won yet incomplete. This was justice, but she still carried the shadow of loss. Keyur and I stood together, lost in a sea of reflection, two friends who had walked through darkness to pay one final respect to her.

The deleted WhatsApp messages were recovered, just as she had said they would be. The CCTV footage that Jason thought he had erased told the story of a calculated murder. Gayatri's voice from beyond the grave had guided us to the truth, and now Jason Thomas would face the consequences of his actions.

As we walked home that evening, the weight of what we had accomplished settled over us. We had been the bridge between the living and the dead, carrying a message that brought justice to a murdered woman. It was no longer just about having a supernatural gift - it was about the responsibility that came with it.

Chapter 3: Nilesh's Last Wish

The sun felt warm on my skin as I left the busy bus stop, my school outfit crisp and fresh from the morning. The familiar sights and sounds of home greeted me, yet an unsettling feeling grew inside me, both comforting and filled with impending worries. I felt drawn to my family home, even though its presence felt burdensome from the start.

The scent of spices transformed as I arrived home, with the familiar kitchen aroma. My mother, Mina, was probably cooking her signature dish, dal, at that moment, because the room smelled delicious, building my anticipation like the simmering pot. At that moment, my father, Prakash, was in a serious discussion about business with a funeral staff member, showing the respect required for our profession.

Once inside, the quiet atmosphere made me notice how the solemn mood of the funeral parlor downstairs had seeped into our home through the floorboards. "Jayesh!" My mum called out to me with her warm voice. I stood by the door, watching as she smoothly stirred the food in the pot with practiced hands. Jasmine fragrance rose naturally from our backyard flowers, blending perfectly with the atmosphere of our home.

From the dining room, I saw my dad deeply immersed in his work, examining a pile of documents with creases on his forehead. Despite his stillness, his eyes conveyed the deep love he felt for me. He turned his head towards me and allowed a hint of pride to shine through his steady expression. He greeted me with a small smile that carried hidden concern.

The quiet moment was interrupted when I responded to my father's greeting with a shifting posture, feeling the weight of the day's experiences settling in. Our quiet voices hung in the air, suspended like a thin string as we faced each other.

Using her kitchen skills, Mina poured hot dal into a bowl and placed it next to cooked rice on the table. She nodded happily but then asked me to assist her in preparing for the temple.

Deep inside, I recognized the importance of these teaching moments but pretended to dismiss their meaning. "Yes, Mum, I'll help. Just let me wash up." As I replied, the nagging feeling entered my stomach, torn between my desire for something higher and the sense that these practices felt like restrictions.

While washing my hands, my mother whispered, "This is our opportunity to reach out to God." The moment carried a lovely message, but instead, it stirred nervousness in me. Meanwhile, Prakash's louder voice stated, "We've brought our dreams and problems to this day." He spoke directly to my mind as if he wanted me to shoulder the burdens everyone faced.

Putting on temple clothes marked the start of our ceremony. Mina wore a flowing red saree for the temple, yet my school clothes felt inadequate for such a sacred moment. The night reminded me that it was time for temple rituals, but I felt unease deep within.

When we arrived at the temple, a mix of spiritual enthusiasm and eager excitement filled the air. The temple sounds echoed between drumbeats, creating a chill that ran through my body. Families followed the same pattern of movement, creating a synchronized dance of faith. The ceremonial diya lights flickered across stone walls, casting separate shadows, while deep inside, a storm raged within me.

In the busy temple, everyone shared their faith, but I couldn't escape my own private sense of loneliness. The thoughts guided me to understand my duties, which blended my gifts and obligations at this age.

I gave myself to prayer while the priests performed their sacred rituals, hoping both my family and I would receive the strength and guidance needed to face our problems. In my thoughts, I imagined my grandmother teaching me about our ancestors' legacy and traditions, reminding me of our heritage and struggles. A strong feeling emerged from within as I sensed the legacy left by those who had passed before me.

After the ceremony ended, we returned home to the funeral parlor where the atmosphere was heavy with the solemnity of our work. Earlier that day, a young boy's body had been delivered to our establishment. The sight of someone so young lying peacefully yet forever still had shaken everyone in our home. My father had worked with quiet reverence, his hands gentle as he prepared the child for his final rest. The boy's name was Nilesh, and seeing someone my age brought a profound sadness that seemed to settle into the very walls of our home.

My father approached me with visible emotions, his normally reserved mask betraying the slightest shift. In a confidential manner, he said, "Nilesh originally owned this item." He passed me a small, polished mobile phone, its metal surface reflecting the faint light of the room. "When my father handed me the phone he said, 'Jayesh, as you know, Nilesh is a young boy. Please keep hold of his phone. He may have a message for his parents.'"

"What?" My thoughts spun as I accepted the item, feeling its weight in my hand. Receiving that phone meant accepting important duties that everyone understood, even without being stated. Prakash kept his eyes fixed on mine, letting his words carry their significance. "From now on, you are the keeper of this object."

Inside, I felt both pleasure and nervousness as I nodded in response. I handled the small device like a historical artifact, staring at it in my fingers. The tiny phone now compared to all the stories and expectations that formed the history of my family.

On my way home, I felt speechless. The bright streetlight's elements passed through my window, casting dark shadows across my disorganized room. The instant I stepped inside, it felt like returning home as I slipped into my personal space, where school books had become worn, and family photos gained new significance.

Mina's jasmine perfume lingered in the room, a reminder of her care for us. A subtle breeze entered through the partially open window, making its way through my mind. Putting down the phone, I paused for a moment to process my emotions.

I uttered my resolution to the empty air before turning my attention to a picture featuring my family members. All the objects in my room, including the cricket ball and the stack of textbooks, seemed to carry the weight of tradition and others' expectations of me.

I went to sleep, the dim light promising future challenges ahead. The phone lay quietly, waiting. My heart pounded, wondering what would happen next, as I faced my responsibilities amid the background of my fears. I drifted to sleep, contemplating my path ahead, choosing to endure the sleepless night before my next journey.

The stillness of my room turned deadly when Nilesh's mobile phone started ringing at 3 AM. The loud, piercing sound shattered the peace, bringing me awake abruptly and speeding up my heart, which still remembered my sleeping thoughts. The peaceful silence in my room turned into a desperate need to act, wrapping around me like fog and pulling me from my peaceful sleep.

My mind went blank when I opened my eyes to dim light, realizing the true situation had reached me. I tried to hush the phone's ringing as I got up from bed, each floorboard creak matching my racing heartbeat. Without thinking, I grabbed the phone from the desk, its light illuminating the space where I had been sleeping. "Hello?" My shaky voice wavered between anxiety and exhaustion.

A faint shaking sound pierced the shadows and reached my ears. "Hello, can you hear me? I need your help." These words, weak yet determined, carried the urgency of the moment. "They're blaming my brother. They say he pushed me." The pressure in my gut rose as the words sank in, pulling me awake from the remnants of sleep.

"What?" I struggled to understand the unfolding situation. My heart beat faster, matching the distress in the caller's voice.

Jayesh asks Nilesh what exactly happened. Nilesh says his story, "I was at the train tracks waiting for a train with my brother Ram. Me and my brother Ram get on very well. Ram is severely autistic but he has a kindness in his heart that no other person has. My laces weren't tied up and my mother told me to tie my shoe laces. I didn't listen to her. The platform was very busy. Ram and I were playing a word game, I spy with my little eye. The platform got more and more busy. As I tried to move a little forward to make more space, I stepped on my shoe laces and fell on the metal train tracks and hit my head." The speaker revealed, "My brother has autism," speaking in a trembling tone. "They're accusing my brother of pushing me because I failed to tie my shoelaces. I just fell. It wasn't my brother's fault. They think because of his autism he pushed me." Nilesh started to cry. I could hear the hurt in his voice. "Please, you must tell my family the truth." My body felt squeezed by the weight of their revelation, the painful truth of their situation seeping in.

Nilesh says, "Please, you need to tell them quickly because they have put my brother Ram in a young offenders home. Ram will not be able to understand what has happened to him. He won't be able to comprehend that I have died and he has been accused. And my mother is going through severe depression. She may do something stupid to herself. They need to get Ram out where he is being held."

As I regained my composure, my words came directly from the pressing situation. "I will try. How old are you?"

He told me his age in a sad, downward tone, his voice that of an 11-year-old. "My older brother, Ram, lives here with me. He's 13."

My body reacted automatically, springing from my seat as I hurried down the stairway, the creaking of each step matching my anxious heartbeat. I reached my parents' room, and the light flashed through the darkened hallway.

"Mum! Dad!" I spoke calmly through barely opened lips as I entered the room. They awoke, startled, their expressions revealing the deep worry etched into their foreheads.

"What's going on?" Prakash mumbled, already sitting up. He appeared in charge, but his protective instincts had kicked in, fatigue creasing his eyes.

"I need your help," I pleaded, explaining Nilesh's terrible story, still fresh in my mind, my words jumbling in a rush of desperation and confusion. Prakash listened carefully, his concerned expression turning into that of a determined leader.

"Alright, first we'll confirm the situation," he commanded, his tone steady. "Ask him deeper questions that only he and his brother would know the answers to."

I hurried back to my room and held the phone firmly, the tension in my palm mirroring the urgency of the situation. "Nilesh?" I looked at the phone and, slowly adopting my father's tone, added, "My next question for you: give me a piece of information only your family knows. It's important."

The line went silent for a few seconds, the tension electric with anticipation. "Alright," he replied weakly, a hint of determination in his tone, doing what no amount of rage could do earlier, making my heart ache. "This is true: my brother and I have a suitcase in the attic with mine and my brother's first baby grows in there. It's a Jungle Book baby grow. One of the baby grows has the third button missing. When I was five, Mum forgot me at the grocery store because her mum, my grandma, was sick and she was stressed. That's when she left me there. When we were little, Mum used to call us 'Ram Lakhan' - it was our nickname from that famous Bollywood movie. Only Mum and Dad know about it."

I almost felt the weight of Nilesh's words, instantly connecting with the family history I had never known. Every detail seemed to connect the boy to another, a hidden current that would draw the two of them into something much bigger than the two of them. And as the words lingered in my mind, I needed reassurance. "What are your mother's and father's names?"

"Nilesh." The word hung in the air, returning to me, coated with both honey and poison. "My mother is Jayshree, and my father's name is Vinod."

When the call ended, the silence in my room felt so thick I could almost cut it with a knife. My parents exchanged a glance, joy mixed with worry and concern in their eyes. As I watched the sunrise, the dawn overpowering the night's gloom, I was overwhelmed with indescribable feelings of obligation.

These thoughts bombarded me: How could one family carry such a burden? What if I couldn't help? But within those fears, there was great resolve, a need to move forward from my own childhood experience into the light of a child's life with a small light bulb.

For a long time, we sat in silence, bearing the weight of the unknown to come. But I felt the flame of determination growing within me. This wasn't just a cry for help; it was a call for change. As morning dawned, bringing limited light into my room, I was ready for what was to come. It was only the beginning of a journey that would alter the lives of a family forever.

Chapter 3: Nilesh's Last Wish Part Two

A significant omen manifested through the early morning cold, which cut through my skin, and the gray sky forecasted the immense burden that approached. The drive to Watford passed in contemplative silence as my father used his reliable shoulders to guide me through both the everyday world and our deep roots in death and mourning. The car wheels made a rhythmic sound as they rolled over the broken pavement, revealing the old brick exterior of Vinod and Jayshree's simple house, standing like an old companion, its stories too painful to recount.

The chilly air carried around the small collection of hedges, facing the seasons with strength, while leaves danced under gentle gusts. Several long shadows belonging to old lampposts served as solemn markers between the past and the forthcoming future. The tension between my father and me increased into a soft yet noticeable pressure that moved silently beneath our mutual lack of communication. Each step he took showed determination, yet his closed lips reflected memories that created permanent facial lines from past disappointments and persistent expectations that held me like a vine, suffocating.

Each furtive movement toward him made my heart increasingly heavier while a weight formed in my chest. My heart pounded with nervousness and resolve as I entered this unfamiliar territory, with a special purpose highlighting both my gift and its embraced obligations. The questions in my mind were whether I could manage this powerful inheritance before collapsing. My unconventional power needed me to use it with the compassion it required.

The entrance stopped me as my hands followed the surface of the heavy wooden door, which bore chipped paint. The door was familiar by its age, since many humans had touched it, along with its pitted brass knocker, which carried the marks of previous stories. My heart raced as I stood there, the heavy atmosphere increasing, and the morning stillness bringing forth the unexpressed emotions between us. My eyes moved to my father, noticing his shoulders rise slightly, as he tried to block the flood of memories that threatened to overwhelm him. A sudden high-pitched tone invaded the air, like a gust of wind, vibrating through my palms before I could determine its source.

When Vinod opened the door, his face showed confusion and wariness. "Who are you?" he asked, his voice thick with exhaustion and grief. Jayshree appeared behind him, her eyes red-rimmed from crying, looking at us with a mixture of hope and suspicion.

"Hello, my name is Prakash and this is my son Jayesh. I am so sorry to disturb you in your hour of grief. I am handling your son Nilesh's funeral preparations." "Oh, OK sure. How can I help you?" said Vinod in a weary voice. "I wonder if we can have a talk with you please." Vinod and Jayshree lead them into the living room. There were photos of Nilesh and Ram on the walls. "How can I help you?" said Vinod. Prakash started by telling Vinod and Jayshree about Jayesh's gift and then how he can communicate with the spirits with the person who died mobile phone.

The change in their expressions was immediate and startling. Vinod's face contorted with anger and disbelief, while Jayshree gasped, her hand flying to her mouth. "That's impossible," Vinod said harshly. "Our son is dead. How dare you come here and, "

"Please," my father interrupted gently but firmly. "We understand how this sounds. But your son contacted us. He's trying to help his brother Ram."

Jayshree's legs seemed to give way, and she leaned heavily against the doorframe. The skepticism in her eyes battled with a desperate hope that perhaps, somehow, this could be real. Vinod still looked at Prakash and Jayesh with anger and curiosity, "How can we believe you," said Vinod. "I have some personal information that Nilesh has told me," Jayesh said, "that in the attic you have a suitcase with Nilesh's and Ram's first baby grows you have kept for sentimental value.

They are Jungle Book baby grows and one of them has its third button missing. And when Nilesh was five years old, auntie he said you forgot him in the grocery store because you were so stressed because your mother was very sick, and you have a loving nickname for Nilesh and Ram you sometimes call them Ram Lakhan from that famous Bollywood movie." After hearing what Jayesh said Vinod nearly fell to the ground.

Jayshree with tears in her eyes, she held my hand and said, "Do you have his phone with you?" "Yes auntie, I do." "Please, can I speak to him please?" Just then my mother's voice came to me in my head. "Jayesh," my mother spoke to me calmly with a strong voice, guiding me through my dark confusion. "You alone can communicate with Nilesh through the phone, so do not give it to anyone else. Only you have the gift. The others will not be able to communicate with him, so keep the phone out of their reach."

"Jayshree bhen," my father said, "only Jayesh can speak to Nilesh's spirit because only he has the gift." Just then Nilesh's phone rang. I answered quickly although my voice faded away. "Hello Nilesh, I am at your house. I am about to speak to your parents." "Can I speak to them please?" said Nilesh in a desperate tone. "They won't be able to hear you Nilesh," I said. "Please Jayesh, please." "They will only be able to hear static Nilesh. I am so sorry."

My chest experienced an intense sensation as she spoke with maternal compassion. "I will take it," I answered quickly, although my voice nearly faded away. My resolution, which had faded, emerged once again with the forceful authority she used to guide me.

I left the hall for a short interval to enter a tiny room with few pieces of furniture, the visible wear on its wooden floor evident. The space smelled of both aged paper and faint sandalwood, while my body felt cold with nervousness. The quick darkening of my eyes allowed me to regain scattered thoughts, yet breathing deeply brought forward haunting memories from my communication with spirits and their bound secrets, along with encounters that felt heavier than the previous ones.

This time, it would be different, I thought to myself, as I tried to suppress the quakes of anxiety that always emerged each time I had to perform unique tasks that only I could do. I felt the cold, hard plastic of the phone in my hand as it offered a focal point that anchored me. After this, with no further impediments ahead, I applied pressure to the device, pressing it to my ear again with much vigor. "You speak to me," I said calmly, though there was uneven stirring inside me, "I will convey it to them." The trusted voice of Nilesh, possessing a tone of request, masked as formal by external audiology.

The following conversation was almost sacred, filled with the weight of intertwining forces that had been far apart for most of the time. It was too late now, and I knew it, the tension, the thrill that ran through their veins as they stepped into this place built upon the sacrifices they made and the dreams that eluded them.

So, when my father and I were coming back into the entrance hall, the morning light mixed with a kind of sinister heat that was rising in my chest. The small house was already there, waiting to become silent while it would hear secrets and stories, pain and despair, hidden for many years, and the frail ray of light that managed to penetrate the darkness.

Entering the gloomy living room felt like getting into a different time, when shadows crawled along the walls and people's secrets moved in between the dust frames, gathering the last gleams of the setting sun. The ornaments were scarce and could hardly convey happiness or affection, instead, they embraced sorrow, memories resonating in a single whisper. This was a sanctuary of sorrow, where every squeak of the floorboards reminded us of everything unsaid and dreams that were never to be realized, the house that Vinod and Jayshree had unknowingly constructed had deeper walls to protect their pain.

There were a lot of things still unsaid, and the silence that enveloped us was as thick as the air we breathed. A couple of familiar armchairs stood like solemn guardians, their exhausted plush inviting anyone who wanted to sit, but nobody in this space shared any stories with them. An old coffee table, too fragile to support the weight of a worn-out embroidered mat placed upon it, embodied fleeting family happiness that once existed long ago. Photographs of families had stuck to the walls, as if the smiles that once illuminated the children's faces had been wiped out, just like the light in the room.

The way Vinod and Jayshree sat made me realize that their suffered souls had bent forward as if hunched over by their loss and sorrow. Their faces morphed into guarded looks of curiosity, turning their gaze in my direction with a hint of sadness that came from unspoken queries. Vinod's eyes were dark, obscured by the darkness of expectation, dampened dreams burning steadily in the darkness of his eyes. Jayshree's eyes welled with unshed tears, and in restless anticipation, she looked for positive feedback on my face.

It was a flood of emotions that surged up, a desire to help them lessen the load of suffering; to convey the words that could recite new scripts for their lives. But there was no time to be intimidated, and as I stared at Vinod and Jayshree with my phone in my hand, I felt the weight of the challenge. Could I tell the truth that would not shatter Jayshree's heart any further?

Gently, I started explaining, "He stressed, Ram had nothing to do with his death; you have to inform the police and get Ram out of jail." I spoke slowly, but distinctly, and my voice pierced through the thick material that hung heavily around us. "Nilesh fell on the train tracks because his shoelaces weren't tied properly. He stepped on his own laces and that's how he fell onto the tracks and hit his head on the metal train tracks." The words I said opened Vinod's eyes, and he saw the truth scrutinized in them. I saw the kind of hope flare in Jayshree's heart and the bleakness fade from her sturdy bearing at the news I brought. The space around us felt confined, everything within it quivering under the weight of what we withheld from each other.

At that instant, all previous arguments burst apart, producing countless open wounds that revealed themselves with agonizing clarity. Shock got the best of Jayshree when she begged through trembling speech for permission to speak with her son. Her words functioned as intense pleas for reconnection with the missing child, while still keeping alive faint validation for salvation.

My heart contracted because of the partitions between life and death. "You cannot directly interact with him, but I will deliver your words for Nilesh to hear." I stated this to Jayshree with quiet understanding. I constructed a thin connection while speaking because every statement reiterated the perpetual loop that split life from death while connecting those in spirit to those still living.

During my conversation, the pictures in my mind showed continuous interactions with spirits from beyond, while each encounter bound together with compassion, grief, and anticipation of salvation. The emotions heightened between us as we felt the profound connection forming.

Vinod all of a sudden started to cry incontrovertibly. "I told him to tie his laces. He always forgot to tie his laces." A sudden understanding struck Vinod, who started crying, his body shaking as pain raged through the air. Jayshree hurried toward me with strong arms to thank me through limited whispered words, which felt like a measure of everything she had lived through. At that moment, she expressed her gratitude through a soft whisper that embraced me with her heat while my body remained cold.

Nilesh's voice emanated through his phone, creating an intense atmosphere in the room and casting a warm glow on Vinod and Jayshree's faces as I spoke his words aloud. "You must dedicate all your affection to Ram, including what I feel for him. I care about Ram at the same depth that both of you share with him. You must find happiness while spending your life with Ram." His moving appeal filled every inch of the room, uniting us in our mourning and shared memories. Jayshree sat next to Jayesh and said, "Please can you tell Nilesh his mother is sitting next to you and please can you hand me the phone? I know he can't hear me. I just want to give him a kiss on the phone. Please tell him what I am going to do." Jayesh told Nilesh his mum was going to kiss him on the phone. Nilesh said to Jayesh, "Please tell her he is going to kiss her and give her a big hug to say goodbye. But please tell her to remember what he had told them." Jayshree took a hold of Nilesh's mobile phone and gave it a motherly kiss and she said, "I love you Nilesh and will miss you so much. We will give Ram all of our love and yours as well," Jayshree sobbing while talking.

Each sincere word caused their expressions to change, as they not only brought me closer to them, but also welcomed the spirits present in the room through the emotional connection between loss and time. "You need peace in your life only by loving Ram completely since he will deeply miss me. Because of his autism diagnosis, he cannot grasp where I have gone. I request you not to inquire about anything further."

The sincere tone of Nilesh's message drowned out the mournful tones, creating a bond between Vinod, Jayshree, and me during this unbreakable moment of mutual exposure.

The sunlight passing through the window illuminated the weak but genuine aspect of our bond. A subtle transformation in the atmosphere appeared when all emotional waves passed, and the tension released itself from my body and mind. The message from Nilesh caused Vinod and Jayshree to let their tears stream down their faces, expressing messages to a lost period of time.

The emotional intensity, combined with deep breaths, made the door to hope slightly broader so warmth could penetrate the gaps. The fragile bond we created inside that living space continued to glow against the harsh exterior environment, marking the beginning of recovery from broken histories.

Two weeks later, Vinod and Jayshree were finally able to bring Ram back home from juvenile prison. The authorities had dropped all charges once the truth about Nilesh's accidental death was revealed through our intervention. When Ram walked through their front door, his face was a mixture of confusion and overwhelming emotion. He immediately looked around the house, searching every room with desperate eyes.

"Where is Nilesh?" Ram asked his mum and dad, his voice trembling with the innocent hope that only someone with his condition could maintain. "Where is my brother?"

Vinod and Jayshree exchanged a look of profound sadness, but also of newfound strength. They would always carry Nilesh's last words in their hearts - his plea to protect Ram and love him with all the affection they had shared between both their sons. With gentle smiles and tears in their eyes, they knelt down to Ram's level.

"He has gone to see God," Jayshree whispered softly, pulling Ram into a warm embrace. "But he will always be watching over us."

And in that moment, as Ram nodded with the trusting acceptance that came so naturally to him, the family began their journey of healing, carrying Nilesh's love and final wishes forward into their future together.

Chapter 4: "Mohini Desai's Secret" Part 1

Between its secret sorrow, in the hushed stillness of the night, the Prakash Family Funeral Parlour exhaled its quiet sighs. And every shadow cradled its sorrow. There was a call on Prakash's phone. Prakash said "OK I am coming down to open the gate." Prakash went downstairs to let the ambulance in, it was another funeral Prakash was going to handle. An hour later Prakash came back upstairs and sat down in the living room. Mina asked him "Is everything OK?" "Yes it's a body of a young woman, Mohini Desai." Prakash put her mobile phone on the coffee table.

The shadows slipped through the narrow spaces of my thoughts, unnoticed by anyone in the world outside. Here, in this sleep-deprived solitude, the walls had voices in them, the voices of souls long dead. The creak of the floorboards kept time with my pulse, a reminder that still life went on here, on the thin edge of impending death. I glanced through the window and saw dim city lights, shining like forgotten stars; they didn't know I carried secrets.

On the table was the phone, lying stark by itself, and I hesitated to let my eyes return to it. A digital phantom called to me from its dull screen, reflecting back at me my apprehension. Was I supposed to answer? It was a weight on my chest, an anchor pulling me deeper into the growing tide of fear. A promise of unfinished business, a connection beyond the veil of life and death, the mobile had come with the body. Mohini Desai. Her name hung heavy in the air.

I closed my fingers around the device, took a breath, and felt the cool weight of it pressed between my palm. It was electric somehow, as if the top floor of this house were soaked in spectral energies. Silence had long since descended, like a funeral shroud, trembling on the verge of breaking. The phone broke the quiet. It rang out, an unholy bell, and I braced myself for the unknown.

Startled, I almost dropped it. "Hello?" My voice was barely above a whisper, as if I might awaken the dead slumbering below. The faint hum of the city outside fell on my ears, a reminder of life, so distant and oblivious to the fact that I was caught in this morbid dance. As the tremor of uncertainty ran through me, I steadied the phone against my ear, aware of the weight of the past cases on my conscience.

Instead of a greeting, there was a voice, and I could tell from the urgency and strain that it was desperate to pull me from the dark vortex. "I really need your help." The voice echoed with despair that curled around my heart. Her words fell into the pit of dread that danced in my mind, a shiver running down my spine, settling there.

"I replied, steadier than I felt, 'Please, tell me how I can help.'" Muffled sounds of her voice started to settle in the shadows of my room, overwhelming me with a story of sorrow and determination. She said her name plainly, arduously realistic, to the point of naivety in spite of where she was. "I am Mohini Desai. I am a widow. Two years ago, my husband, Mukesh, died of cancer."

Her revelation, suffocating and captivating, was as heavy as a lead blanket on my shoulders. Mukesh's life unfolded in her voice, stories of mundane success, a man who had mapped himself through three supermarkets in Radlett. Each word she spoke wove together strands of loss and pain, but the threads slipped between her fingers as the shadow of her cousin, Priyesh, loomed over her story.

She hesitated for a second before continuing. "When my husband passed away, I needed help with my husband Mukesh's shops. I had a cousin in India who Mukesh and I were close to; his name is Priyesh. My husband had already sent him a work permit so he could get a visa from India to give him some much-needed help in the shops.

Priyesh came from India to help me after my husband passed away, to help with Mukesh's shops. Priyesh was very helpful, looking after everything. He was very good with my two sons, the eldest is Bipin, who is 9 years old, and the youngest is Davey, who is 7 years old. Priyesh was like a brother to me and my sister Mayuri, who lives with her husband Trevor in Leicester.

But after a while, I could see little changes in Priyesh, the way he started to talk rudely with the other staff in the shops. His own choices were getting more and more extravagant; he had bought a new Range Rover car. I told my sister Mayuri and brother-in-law Trevor. They both said he works hard and wants to buy nice things, so I didn't take much notice after that.

But one evening, my accountant rang me and said, 'Mohini, I have found some discrepancies in the accounts. I need to come to see you urgently.' He told me not to tell Priyesh about our meeting but to please tell your sister Mayuri and her husband Trevor to come. I will come tomorrow evening.

I called Mayuri and Trevor; they were both wondering, like I was, what this could be. When my accountant came to the house the next day, he told us about how Priyesh had been skimming money out of the business. My accountant said he hadn't told me earlier because he had to be sure. He said Priyesh had taken around fifty thousand pounds.

Me, Mayuri, and Trevor were stunned." Jayesh's heart raced as she described Priyesh's treachery and the plotting of an almost unimaginable plan.

Mohini's voice grew more intense with every minute. She said, "Me, my sister Mayuri, and brother-in-law Trevor did some digging and found out Priyesh had started to gamble heavily." Suddenly, she broke away from her story and said, "You must please call the police. Priyesh has had my son Davey kidnapped. Please, please, please," Mohini said hysterically.

Jayesh couldn't believe what he was hearing. He told Mohini, "Please don't worry. I am only 13 years old. Please let me get my mum and dad." "Please hurry," shouted Mohini.

Jayesh quickly ran down to the living room, where his mum Mina and dad Prakash were watching a movie. "Mum, Dad," shouted Jayesh, holding the phone high in his hand, "Mohini's phone rang. I have been speaking to her."

Mina held Jayesh's hand and said, "OK, calm down, son. Tell us what she said." Jayesh told his parents about Mohini's husband, who passed away a few years ago, their shops in Radlett, and about Priyesh. He explained what her accountant had told Mohini, her sister Mayuri, and brother-in-law Trevor about Priyesh stealing money, and how Mohini told him her son Davey had been kidnapped.

"OK, son," said Prakash, "turn the phone on and speak to her again. We need to act fast. Relay every word Mohini says to us."

Jayesh turned the phone back on and spoke. "Hello, Mohini, are you there?" "Yes, I am here," she said.

"Mohini, my parents are here. I have told them what you told me. Dad is going to ask you questions through me."

Prakash told Jayesh to ask Mohini to continue her story about Priyesh from where she left off because they needed more information. Mohini said, "OK."

She explained, "Priyesh heard about the conversation with the accountant because Priyesh had Mohini's living room bugged and her phone bugged." She spoke very quickly and anxiously, "Priyesh has lots of friends. He got three of them to kidnap my son, who wanted to walk home from school with his friend."

I could hypothetically feel Mohini's tears on my shoulder as she cried uncontrollably. Mohini said, "I didn't know he had my room and phone bugged. When Davey didn't come home from school, I was so worried I called the police, and my sister Mayuri and brother-in-law came straight away."

At night, they had a call from the kidnappers. They said they had Davey and wanted five hundred thousand pounds. "We never thought in our wildest imagination that Priyesh would do this."

The kidnappers said Davey was safe and wouldn't be hurt unless they got the money. They said they had until 5 pm the next day to call again and give instructions on where to leave the money. They told me not to tell anyone, not to phone the police, and not to tell any family member.

After the phone call from the kidnappers, Priyesh burst into tears. I was stupidly consoling him. Trevor said, "Don't worry

Mohini, I can get the money in the morning." Trevor was a financial expert.

Priyesh said he had some money in India he could get here tomorrow. He hugged me and Mayuri, and we did feel comforted by Priyesh. We genuinely thought he wanted to help because he was very close with his nephews.

Priyesh said he would make us some strong Indian masala tea to help us think straight. He went into the kitchen and made the tea. After we drank our tea, Priyesh convinced us all to get some sleep to be fresh in the morning. How silly we were to fall into his trap.

Priyesh had put poison in my cup of tea so that when I fell asleep, I wouldn't wake up and it would look like I had a heart attack. The police would think I had a heart attack because I was worried about Davey being kidnapped.

Jayesh couldn't believe what he was hearing. With every new piece of news, his pupils dilated. Her story extended further to the point of horror.

Mohini said, "Please, you need to go quickly and see my sister and brother-in-law. They are at my house in Radlett helping to find Davey. My eldest son Bipin is so upset. He has lost both parents, and his brother has been kidnapped."

"My sister and brother-in-law will give Bipin all the love me and Mukesh could have given him." She swallowed her words, and her fear was loud and clear, a crescendo louder than the silence of the room.

The desperation in her voice intensified as she continued, "I need your help, please."

As I relayed every word Mohini told me to my parents, my mum Mina squeezed my hand tighter. "Please tell her not to worry. We will go and see Mayuri and Trevor and get them to call the police."

Mohini interrupted me by saying, "You must get them to do an autopsy so they know I have been poisoned. Priyesh has thrown the poison in the lake, but you will be able to get evidence from his phone because he ordered the poison from his friends in India."

Prakash asked Mohini, "Where are they holding Davey?"

Mohini, with a loud and desperate voice that only I could hear, said, "They have taken him to a disused garage in Birmingham."

Mohini gave us the address.

My thoughts raced, and I fell onto the wall to catch my breath. Suddenly, the reality of the situation got a hold of me. I said, "A young boy's life is on the line. Get a grip, Jayesh!"

Mina, my mother, looked at me with a reassuring look and said, "Don't worry son, we are here with you."

I could feel the walls beginning to close in as I thought about the task ahead. This caused me to feel the dread rising as the gears moved slowly, connecting all the points in the fabric of my life with thin threads of the supernatural.

My forced walk to the other side, a side where no one my age should be, was something I knew deep inside me I was doing good.

I went to my room to lie down for a few minutes to get some normality in my head, but I couldn't get Mohini's voice out of my mind. Her voice got stuck in my mind, etched with a clear engraving of all that Mohini had uttered, gripping fear, violence, death, and betrayal.

It appeared I had been caught in a web far more complicated than I had ever imagined. My hands shook against my thighs, kneading the wooden texture of the table as I realized the severity of Mohini's suffering.

So began the realization of the links running through me. My family history was thick with us. What did I truly inherit? Not just the funeral parlour but something far more nebulous and sinister than that.

It wasn't merely a process meant to pay respect to the dead; it was a method to interpret the meaning, the cues left by the departed.

I was only 13, but I had obligations and duties to perform for the spirits and families left behind to ease their grief.

During my early days, I struggled to accept my natural skills, passed down from my ancestors. They pushed me to act now because my fear was trying to stop me.

I knew contacting Mayuri and Trevor was vitally important, much more important than fear.

My father came to me and said, "Jayesh, we need to move fast. How would I manage if this situation was too much for me?"

I said to my dad, "I am right next to you, so you don't need to be frightened. I won't let anything happen to you."

He was always a pillar of strength for me.

Given that Mohini's children needed saving, I had to stay focused.

Mina got up from her chair and said, "Come on, we need to act fast. We can't just sit around thinking too much."

Prakash, my father, said, "Jayesh, you need to ask Mohini something personal about her that only Mohini and her sister Mayuri would know. We can't just turn up uninvited and tell them you are speaking to spirits. They will call the police on us."

Mina said, "Yes, your father is right, Jayesh. Please ask her."

I took Mohini's phone and switched it on again. I put the phone to my ear and called out her name, "Mohini, are you there?"

"Yes," she said.

Mohini spoke to us about her secret. She said, "I have a secret that only Mayuri and I know. Not even Mayuri's husband Trevor knows what I am about to tell you."

Mohini hesitated a little.

Jayesh said, "What is it?"

"I don't know if I should be telling a boy your age this, but my son's life is in jeopardy, so I will tell you."

"When Mayuri was 16 years old, she was in the fifth form at school. I was 2 years above her in upper sixth form. Mayuri was going out with a boy in her year, and a long story short, Mayuri got pregnant."

"I was so angry with her. My parents didn't know about this. I was 18 years old, so I was old enough to be her guardian."

"She had an abortion, and only Mayuri and I know about this."

"But Jayesh, when you or your dad tell her about this, please don't say anything in front of her husband Trevor. He may know about this. Mayuri must have told him, but just in case, tell her privately please."

Prakash said, "Let me give Mohini's sister Mayuri a call to ask her where she is. I have her number because she called me to look after the funeral preparations."

"Just go to Mohini's house in Radlett. You don't need to call her. Please leave quickly," said Mina impatiently.

"But they may have gone back to Leicester to their own home."

Mina said with a stern voice, "Why would they go back to Leicester when her nephew has been kidnapped, for God's sake?"

Prakash said angrily, "It's better to be safe than sorry."

Prakash dialed Mayuri's number and said, "Mayuri, this is Prakash from Prakash's Funeral Parlour. We need to come and see you and your husband Trevor. Is that OK?"

"Yes, sure. Is everything OK?" asked Mayuri.

"Yes, we just need a quick chat in person with you. Is that OK?"

"Sure, no problem. We are at my sister's house in Radlett."

"OK, fantastic. See you shortly. Thanks."

"Come on, Jayesh, let's go," Mina said, giving Prakash a hug. "I am so sorry, my darling. I got angry at you. It's because I'm getting so worried about Davey."

"Don't worry, Mina. It's OK."

Prakash again told Jayesh, "Quickly, son, we have to go."

Jayesh hesitated a little and said, "Dad, can we take Keyur with us?"

Keyur was Jayesh's best friend. He knew all about Jayesh's gift and had been alongside him on other adventures.

"OK, sure. Call him. We will pick him up on the way."

Jayesh told Keyur everything that had happened. He rang Keyur already and told him.

They got to Keyur's house, which was only round the corner from Jayesh.

Keyur got in the car and said hello to Prakash and gave Jayesh a mischievous grin, "Another body and another mystery."

Chapter 4: "Mohini Desai's Secret" Part Two

Keyur was talking about the Premiership football match on TV yesterday, trying to lighten the mood in the car. Jayesh wasn't really listening to Keyur; he was getting very nervous the nearer they got to Mohini's house.

Each bump from the road to the other side of Radlett made me tense because it reminded me of the difficult path that lay before us. My father knew where Mohini's house was because they lived in the same town we did, Radlett. Radlett was quite a large town; they lived on the other side of Radlett.

When the car stopped next to Mohini's home, a dark feeling formed an invisible garment that made the air heavier in our vehicle. I glanced at my dad and Keyur and saw their matching feelings of concern because we all feared what lay ahead.

As we drove up to Mohini's house, Mayuri and Trevor came outside. They must have heard our car from inside the house. They stood awaiting us while concealing their feelings until meeting our eyes. Mayuri greeted us as she talked with a strained voice.

"Hello Prakash, how are you? What brings you all here?"

"I am well, thank you Mayuri. So sorry to disturb you in your hour of grief. May we have a chat with you both, please?"

"Yes, sure," said Mayuri. "Please come in."

As we went into the kitchen, we sat around the dining table.

"OK, how can I help you?" said Mayuri. "Do your sons want to play in the garden while we speak?"

"No, it's OK. They need to be here too."

Prakash spoke quickly because the information he wanted to give weighed heavily upon me.

"I need to talk to you both. It's very important."

My rapid heartbeat grew as my father started to tell them about my gift and how I could communicate with the spirits that came into his funeral parlour. He told them all about how I could talk to the spirits through the mobile phones of the deceased.

"We had a call on Mohini's phone from her. The spirits only try to contact Jayesh, my son, if their soul is disturbed about something."

Trevor got up and said, "So are you telling me that my sister-in-law Mohini has been in contact with your son through her own mobile phone?"

"Yes, please you need to listen to us. It's very important."

Mayuri looked at Jayesh with complete hatred in her eyes.

"Please listen to what we have to tell you, please."

Just then Jayesh spoke.

"Look, Mayuri auntie, I have some private information Mohini told me about you, but she told me to tell you in private."

Mayuri gave a sarcastic laugh.

"OK, what information do you have about me? Go on, tell me," Mayuri was getting more and more irritated.

Jayesh said, "Mohini told me to tell you in private, please."

"No! You can tell me in front of my husband! I have nothing to hide!"

Prakash said, "OK, if you want me to tell you, I will. It's about you getting an abortion when you were 16 years old."

Mayuri's face went white.

"How the hell did you know this?"

"Mohini told me."

Mayuri and Trevor looked at Prakash and Jayesh in disbelief, and you could see they started to believe us.

Prakash said quickly, "Look, this is not about you, Mayuri. We know all about the kidnapping of Davey, your nephew. Look, we know where Davey is being held. Saving Davey is the most important thing at the moment, please."

Mayuri and Trevor's tone changed. Now you could see they really believed me and my dad.

"But look, there is more to this. You need to listen carefully. Your cousin Priyesh from India instigated the whole kidnapping. He got three of his friends to help him.

"We know Priyesh is a big gambler and is in a lot of debt. Your sister told us, Mayuri, that the accountant told Mohini that Priyesh has been skimming money from her business for a long time. And he has been using Mohini's money to fund his lavish lifestyle.

"Priyesh has got the living room bugged and the telephone line bugged. That's why he had Davey kidnapped. But please sit down; you have to listen to the worst part. Priyesh poisoned Mohini."

"What!!" said Mayuri.

"That night when you got a call from the kidnappers about the five hundred thousand pounds ransom, Priyesh offered to make you all a cup of strong Indian masala tea, am I right?" said Prakash.

"He put the poison in Mohini's cup."

Trevor and Mayuri were absolutely broken up inside.

Trevor said, "How can we prove this?"

"Look, first of all, let's rescue Davey. He is being held in a disused garage in Birmingham. It's an industrial estate in a town in Birmingham called Handsworth.

"We need to get an autopsy done on Mohini's body. We need the detectives to take Priyesh's phone and go through it because it is evidence of him sending messages to his friends in India to buy him the poison.

"Mohini said he has dumped the poison in a lake, but his phone has evidence. But most importantly, we can't let Priyesh get any idea of what we are doing because he can have Davey killed."

Trevor said, "OK, we need a plan. We need to call the investigating detective on his mobile and meet him at the police station. We can't let him come here because Priyesh may find out."

I pleaded, "We have to go to the police now!!"

I let the desperation in my tone spill out in my voice.

Silence took over, and I could almost taste the tension in the atmosphere. Their delay was obvious.

That was the moment that reinforced that we would not live in fear, that we would not let our fears drive us.

I needed them to understand how important my plea was, that our collective trauma had been forged in an unyielding bond, incomplete without the justice that could no longer be denied.

Mayuri and Trevor got in the car with Prakash, Jayesh, and Keyur.

In the car, Prakash tells Mayuri and Trevor, "Look, we can't tell the detective about Jayesh's gift that he can speak to the spirits. They won't take us seriously."

They got to the police station, and Detective Inspector Spencer was waiting for them outside.

They went in and told the inspector everything, all about where Davey was being held, how Priyesh instigated the kidnapping, and how he poisoned Mohini.

They said they needed to get an autopsy done and find evidence in Priyesh's phone.

Detective Spencer sprang into action.

Mayuri gave him the address where Davey was being held.

The detective called for a helicopter.

Mayuri and Trevor asked if they could come because Davey would be so frightened, and seeing his auntie and uncle would be comforting for Davey.

The detective said, "Of course you can."

Just then Mayuri asked if we could come too.

"Sure, no problem," said the detective, "but just keep out of the way please."

We all went to the helicopter pad and got in the helicopter.

Keyur and I had never been in a helicopter, but our excitement was overtaken by thinking of the rescue mission for young Davey.

Like a mouth, the garage loomed before me, its walls were a black, worn, and cracked mouth, dripping with secrets they were not saying.

Officers entered methodically and grim-faced, their expressions unburdened by the emotional weight that I sunk into my bones.

Hope, glistening like the light of a day lost, shone in the shadows of the place.

The officers moved patiently, their movements precise, as if coming to one accord in the language of their profession.

The tension in the air was heavy, and each creak of the floorboards and scrape of shoes against gravel only made it tenfold heavier.

The stink of oil, rust, and musty scents engulfed me; only breathing seemed a betrayal to the times.

From a murky space, I heard a shout from one of the officers. My heart hammered.

"Over here!"

The dim illumination shone on their faces; they clustered near a corner of littered debris and broken light fixtures.

The moment I realized they were approaching their discovery filled me with desperate hope.

There was Davey, a fragile figure between the detritus of human neglect, slumped in a corner.

Relief and horror hit all at once, like becoming frozen in an icy wave.

I took a step back to remind myself that this was real, that there was something still to fight for.

The officer yelled, "Stay back," while clearing the path forward to conduct scene security before activating the emergency response system.

The collision of my thoughts brought me to wonder if hope had any chance to survive in that desperate situation.

My emotions fought against protocol as Davey met my eyes because I desperately wanted to rescue him from the mourning silence, but the professional boundaries prevented my actions.

Mayuri and Trevor ran to Davey.

Davey ran to Mayuri and hugged her so tight, crying.

Mayuri couldn't hold back her tears; she started to cry, holding Davey in her arms.

"Oh my little baby, my little sweetheart," Mayuri was gasping for breath; she was crying so much.

Prakash had tears rolling down his cheeks.

I even saw tears in the eyes of Detective Inspector Spencer as well.

A sudden change in the scene grew more fearsome when we entered the bright and sterile examination room, which exposed every surface through harsh fluorescent lighting.

A clinical feel pervaded the area, which before had been flooded with warmth and now acted as the stage for Mohini's tragic poisoning.

The autopsy process started with forensic experts who conducted their tasks with detached aptitude and both gloved and expressionless faces.

Every new cut in her body became an accidental reminder of the horrifying events we faced.

Their precise peeling motions revealed the truth: Mohini died of poisoning because of their careful analysis of her body.

The realization of what happened caused tears to form at the edge of my eyes.

The search for explanations had led us to discover pain through betrayal and loss which tormented the core of my being.

A different scene unfolded before us.

The police had told Priyesh to come to Mohini's house because they needed his help.

Detective Inspector Spencer was very careful so that Priyesh didn't suspect anything.

As soon as Priyesh got out of his brand-new Range Rover, police handcuffed him and took his mobile phone to analyze.

But as the handcuffs clicked around his wrists, Priyesh's composure finally cracked.

His eyes darted wildly between the officers and then landed on me with a mixture of rage and disbelief.

"How the hell did they find out?" he shouted, his voice breaking with panic.

"How could you possibly know? There's no way... no one knew!"

His shock was genuine, his confusion complete.

The man who had orchestrated such careful betrayal couldn't comprehend how his web of lies had unraveled.

The officers guided him toward the police car, his voice still echoing in the air.

"How did you find out? How?"

Mayuri and Trevor went to the police car where Priyesh was put and shouted, "How can you have done this? My sister gave you everything. Why did you have to kill her?"

Priyesh just looked out of the police car window and then hung his head in shame.

Detective Inspector Spencer came up to Mayuri and Trevor and said, "Can I ask you two questions please? How did you find out the address where Davey was being held, and how did you know Mohini was poisoned?"

Mayuri looked at the detective and said while sobbing, "What does it matter? My sister has gone."

Trevor and Prakash put their arms around Mayuri.

Prakash said, "You have your sister's boys to bring up now."

Which is when Mayuri said with a smile, looking at the sky, "I will love them just as my sister did."

Mayuri gave Jayesh and Keyur a great big hug and said, "You are my hero, Jayesh. We will never forget what you have done for us."

In the car on the way home, no one said a word, but they all had a look of great achievement for what was done today.

When they got home, Prakash told Mina all about it.

Jayesh just went straight to his room and fell asleep.

Chapter 5: "The Skeptic's Challenge"

Darkness spread throughout our small house, meeting every wall with its thick shadows. The tranquility ended when the phone rang loudly through the empty space. From my room upstairs, I could hear the phone ringing downstairs. I couldn't concentrate on my homework - I was eagerly awaiting a challenge from a new body.

My heartbeat sounded an alarm as Dad answered the phone. The editor, Pankaj Patel, spoke into Dad's ear with sharp words that cut straight to his heart. He spoke fast and excitedly because secrets about his son had caught his attention. Pankaj told Dad there was a remarkable story about how his son Jayesh displays unbelievable abilities. I am a friend of Mohini the lady who's funeral preparations you looked after, me Mohini and Mayuri were in the same school. Trevor and Mayuri mentioned it. The rumor holds that he possesses this remarkable gift. The reality of his statement created severe pain in Dad's stomach.

"Of course not! What makes you repeat worthless rumors?" Dad's sudden interruption stabbed through the atmosphere with his strong voice. Prakash knew Pankaj Patel was an editor for a Punjabi Indian newspaper in Southall and was angling for a story for his paper. The fury built up in his throat, turning sour like spoiled food. The editor pressed his point in a stricter voice. "Look Prakash, I am going to print a story

- it is better if I can get your side of the story. Prakash, I know you quite well. I handled your advertise in my paper when you started your funeral parlour all those years ago. I just want to get your side of the story." The idea alone made Dad's ventricles race inside his body.

As their conversation continued, Dad's emotions worsened until they threatened to explode like a building storm. "It's a family matter, Pankaj." Dad's response stopped, but the editor's words continued to stand true. People in our community had passed gossip to him for a long time. Listening to him speak it in such a direct manner felt like our privacy had been breached.

After releasing his breath, Dad put down the phone, his fingers resting on the handset. His gaze turned toward Mina, who patiently examined the situation with her eyes. She decided to face reality, so people would discover our secret. She carried heavy acceptance with her words that penetrated Dad's mind.

Dad released a long breath that ended like the last air remaining in a flat balloon. At that moment, he let Mina guide him by holding his gaze into hers. "Bring him home for us to discuss what he wants to tell." The thought of meeting our reality brought Dad deep dread along with the need to defend our hidden life.

The living room took on funeral parlor qualities because it held old furniture that stored numerous unspoken tales along with our family establishment's faded logo visible from the large window. Every part of the room prepared for battle as Pankaj Patel walked through the entrance, increasing the tension with his arrival.

He entered the space with his posture stiff and watchful, while the home felt welcoming. Dad observed him scrutinize the room and stay too long checking out the photos on display, which captured memories of individuals who passed away. Pankaj was acting like a detective. The detective stared at the scene with a cruel look because he wanted to find the hidden truth. Dad sensed that both of them had to stay in complete control during this situation.

Dad's body remained tight and still against the side of the shelf because he waited to face his examination. The room seemed tight because its walls appeared to crush us like a trap. Dad protected the secrets from beyond while keeping the world of the living separate. His hands shook faintly next to his body as his inner fear threatened to break through.

Jayesh and Keyur showed their intensity by standing near. The boys glimpsed each other, and their expressions shone with eagerness, they were two boys eager to explore without seeing our hidden problems. Dad's feelings blended protection with happiness because he saw them rest in the magic before noticing any danger.

"Could you describe the special talents your son exhibits?" Pankaj asked his questions in both caring and pushy tones. His gaze landed on Jayesh right away as though he wanted to unveil our secrets from our family.

Dad felt the rhythm of his heartbeat threatening to give away his secret position. He understood the full effect this tale might have when shared.

Dad spoke his answer with determination. "The public needs to stay away from this matter." Everyone felt an electric energy amounting to a storm about to explode because Dad's cheeks started burning. Pankaj's observing gaze wore down Dad's determination until he had to confront what really happened with both of them.

Dad's little comfort habits gave away his distress through his clenched hand and firm jaw as he tried not to let anybody see his son. Pankaj continued, determined, pressing deeper. The inquiries from Pankaj caused greater discomfort than intended, so Dad had to focus on his good intentions.

Our conversation progressed back and forth until the room became hollow with quiet that pushed us toward revealing important facts. Jayesh fidgeted in his seat when Keyur looked at him through youthful remorse that recalled his carefree nature. Dad struggled to keep the peace between us as guilt and shame started growing inside him again. Our truths floated through the room, making us question our established life.

Pankaj raised his face as he leaned forward with his book lying on his knee in the position of a predator about to strike. "According to reports, your son holds a remarkable ability. Your child's talent needs to be shared with everyone."

Mina took Dad's hand gently, feeling his hot temperature contrasted with hers. We found comfort from her handhold, which helped us survive when life was hard. Dad said firmly, "It's important to focus on what benefits our son above what the world should receive. Our highest priority lies in doing what serves our kid best."

A brief knockback of the light above us made shadows on our walls that followed our unknown worries. Morning sandalwood incense blended with dust and book scent drifted through the air to join the chemical tinge on Dad's clothing, which brought back memories of his downstairs tasks as a mortician.

"Dad," Jayesh's voice came from his side, startling as it was confident and firm for a boy of thirteen years. "I had glimpsed the possibility of serendipity, and I was intent on experiencing it again; so I said to him, 'I don't mind talking about it.'"

These five words arrested the air in the room, as people breathed in and waited to exhale. The following line suggests turning to the child in the narrative and seeing his eyes as containing the richest knowledge that is usually associated with elders: This new life burdened the cradle of my generations as Dad eyed him, this child between two worlds he still knew little about.

"Jayesh," Dad said as the danger in his voice should have been obvious, but Jayesh looked him right in the eyes.

"I only hear the spirits when they contact me on their own mobile phone," Jayesh went on saying, now turning to Pankaj. "Some spirits have a matter that is troubling them - that's why their soul can't get peace. They will call and that's how I can hear them." His admission lingered in the silence that followed.

Keyur nodded enthusiastically beside him. "I can't hear the spirits - only Jayesh can. When Jayesh asks for private information about the deceased family which only the deceased and the family members know, and we go and see - it's completely accurate. No one could know that information."

Many times, Pankaj took his pencil and scribbled his notes high on ideas in a manner that seemed exhilarated. "And what do these voices say to you, Jayesh?"

Dad opened his arms about to interrupt, but then Mina took a grip of his hand. The look that she gave him in the eye was pleading with him to be more cautious. The words of war that he had wanted to say and the urge to spill the secrets in order to free himself were fighting within him as well.

"They say that they are still alive," Jayesh managed to whisper back. "They need someone to listen. Someone to help them finish what they left undone."

The confession appeared to change the atmosphere of the room and filled it with tension that made the hairs on Dad's arms stand up. Pankaj looked at both of them for a while, assessing, analyzing the significance of this information against his professional convictions.

Finally, Pankaj wanted to know how long it has been occurring. "How long has this been happening?" he pressed, leaning closer.

"As far as I can remember," responded Jayesh, whose shoulders were clearly pulling back with a kind of pride that was both inspiring and fear-inspiring to Dad. "After Rumesh contacted me first. He was the first spirit I heard from."

Dad could see his father's face as clearly as if he were standing in front of him; he had been strict but caring, his hands gripping Dad's as he tried to teach him the profession of their trade. Mourning customs, cremation, and other methods that had been used to give the dead some form of preparation to move to the next sphere. The business had always been inherited by each successive generation of their family. Their house is literally built on top of the funeral home, as a daily reminder of life's fragility.

"That's enough," Dad whispered, for reasons he would later regret as his voice betrayed him, leaving him sounding like a man with no water and little sleep for the past few days, which wasn't far off from the truth. "Pankaj, you should go."

However, the editor continued to concentrate on his son. "Have you ever helped them? The spirits who speak to you?"

Dad was still wondering how he was going to keep them from making such a decision when Jayesh approached them, and immediately, his face became serious. "I remember a woman last month. She could not rest because her daughter was unable to locate where she had concealed her wedding ornaments. I told Dad, and he..."

"Jayesh," Dad said threateningly, but before he could complete his words, the deed had been done. The story was out, so to speak, like smoke dispersed in the air, which cannot be caught once again.

"You helped me find the daughter," Jayesh started uttering these words, his voice trembling with courage. "We told her where to look. Behind the loose brick in the kitchen wall. As she was instructed, she searched and found her mother's gold there."

Pankaj's eyes opened wide and he looked at Dad as if in anticipation of hearing the answer from him. There was some noise from the cars passing by and the rhythmic noise coming from the grandfather clock in the corner, a family relic that had seen many secrets over the years.

"Is this true?" He asked this at last, and in his tone, Dad could understand that the words he spoke should be spoken with absolute respect.

Dad let out a breath and immediately felt the spirit of all the other Patel Funeral Directors suffocating him. His ancestors, who always existed between the domain of the living ones and the domain beyond it. Perhaps some had known, deep down, more than they cared to let on regarding the murmurs that sometimes arose concerning their job.

"Yes," Dad said, feeling the word stuck and croaky. "It's true."

It was uttered as if the truth were lying right between them and nothing could be done to change it. Dad felt an odd feeling of relief as well as a new weight bear upon him. The secret was revealed at least in part. What was left to be proved was, how the world would accept it and whether the life that he was trying to build, brick by brick, would survive the attempts to dismantle it.

Mina's grip tightened her fingers around Dad's, and just like a current of strength ran through her entire body. Whatever came next, they would face it together, as they had faced all other spiritual murmurs that wiggled their way into their home in the many years of spirits passing through their dwelling downstairs.

"Speak," said Pankaj very seriously as he held a pencil above the notepad. "From the beginning."

Dad drew a big sigh, as if taking a big breath that could fill him with as much courage as he could manage.

Prakash told Pankaj about Mina's family legacy, the gift that has been handed down through generations.

Mina interrupted by saying, "My mother Manorama, Jayesh's grandmother, and my sister have all got spiritual gifts. My mother told me that her mother had a gift as well."

Prakash said, "Jayesh never asked for this. He is a normal 13-year-old boy. I saw how this gift had taken hold of Jayesh. I was so frightened and amazed by how my son has used this gift to give peace to spirits who can't go to their final resting place because there is something disturbing their soul, and how Jayesh has helped their families come to terms with their grief.

Pankaj, I have tried to protect my son, but now this gift he has is out in the open. I am worried about how the Asian community will look at my son. I don't want you to write something in your newspaper that will make a laughing stock out of my son. Pankaj, you should ask your friends Mayuri and Trevor how Jayesh has helped them."

You could see the raw emotion on Prakash's face.

Mina said, "You are an editor of a newspaper and just want to sell your newspapers. You do not know anything about the environment we live in. Of course, I know you are a skeptical person, Pankaj. But please don't make a mockery of our profession when you write your article."

Mina bhen said, "Pankaj, I am sorry if I have come across rude. That was not my intention. I know how Prakash's funeral parlour has helped so many families with their funeral preparations.

Please don't worry. I will find out all the facts before I write my article, and I will show you both before it goes to press."

Prakash got up and shook Pankaj's hand and said, "Thank you."

Pankaj said in a joking manner, "One day, hopefully, you will look after my funeral preparations."

With that, they all had a good laugh.

Chapter 5: "The Skeptic's Challenge" Part Two

Pankaj asks Prakash, **"Can we please go down to your funeral parlour? I just want to see where the bodies come in."**

"Why do you need to see that?" asked Prakash.

"But okay, no problem, I will take you."

It was a dusky room that was located in the basement of Dad's business, with a smell of lumber polish, decaying into the background of the hollow memories of the parlour. Dad sat down behind his mahogany desk, which was made for his father. Prakash glared from behind the heaps of yellowing ledger books and the framed portraits of people whose funerals Prakash had taken care of in the past.

"Come on, tell me," Pankaj said, getting closer to Prakash, clenching the edge of the desk before him. **"How is your son contacting the dead?"**

The question echoed aloud and reverberated around the room, silencing everyone. Dad's gaze fell to the dull floral pattern of the carpet.

"Please tell me, Prakash. Everyone needs to know about Jayesh's gift."

Pankaj, now puffed up and scowling, crossed his arms.

"Look, Prakash, I need to write an article about this. I can't give up this opportunity for this unbelievable story. I'm going to print this, it's my job."

"Yes, as I said, I can do that with your assistance so it can be turned into a good article."

"Look," Prakash said to Pankaj, "we don't want any headlines. We really don't want to be in your paper. Jayesh is only thirteen years old. He is just a young boy. My son will not know what it's like in our Asian community to be exposed to the gossiping of people in our society."

Just then, Mina walked into the room.

"The dilemma we have is, Pankaj bhai," said Mina, "that we are trying to protect my son, and once word gets out about his gift, we will be inundated with calls and visitors. Prakash's funeral parlour is very famous in England because he handles a lot of funerals from the Asian community from all over the country. Once the article is published, everyone will know about Jayesh's gift."

A barely discernible outline entered the area flooded by the desolate fluorescent light, and then Mina appeared before them. In a more subdued manner, it was a rather tender hand that laid itself on Prakash's arm.

"Mina said, 'Pankaj, this gift has been handed down in generations in my side of the family. As I told you before, my mother Manorama and my sister both have the gift,' which sounded like a statement of fact, as well as a plea for continuity of her heritage."

"Please tell me how they contact Jayesh," Prakash said.

"The spirits communicate with Jayesh through their own mobile phones. Not all spirits find Jayesh, only when they've been troubled and cannot rest."

Prakash spoke without any emotion in his voice, and his gaze moved around the room as if he was seeking support from the things that belonged to their ancestors.

And there Jayesh stood in his small form, with words enveloping him as he remained silent.

Without showing much personal interest, Pankaj asked Jayesh, "Okay, when do they contact you? Do you have a feeling or something?"

The atmosphere became heavy with anticipation, while all sounds around them ceased in that instant. The pressure became intense because Jayesh wanted to break the silence where his thoughts normally stayed.

Jayesh spoke, **"I speak through the mobile phones of the deceased to receive their messages. Not every deceased person contacts me; sometimes I don't get any contact for a few months. Pankaj uncle, let's do this. I will ask my father to call you when I receive contact from a spirit."**

Prakash looked at Jayesh with astonishment.

"Okay, fantastic, Jayesh, that will be fantastic," said Pankaj.

Prakash delivered his words in a serious yet optimistic manner when he asked, **"Is that acceptable, Pankaj? Hold off on your reports until you observe the contents firsthand. After you witness everything, you can put your pen to paper and write your article."**

Tension hung delicately throughout the space, which built an eternal connection between all of them while both parties carried significant burden and dread over potential revelation.

Pankaj maintained his stare to study Prakash with wonder, yet he made a clear promise that a story would emerge later.

The editor left with a somber expression after his departure, creating an ambiance of hidden emotion and equipment noise which filled the space. When he moved through the room, his polished shoes made sounds on the floor that conveyed their vulnerable state and the tricky process they maintained between doubtful attitudes and accepted inheritance.

Fluorescent light clashed with dark shadows to create an uncertain lighting effect, which symbolized their internal fight. This funeral parlor represented both a shelter for their truths and a platform for hidden secrets that yearned for validity.

After the heavy door sealed, Prakash experienced the repercussions of his exit, which reminded him about their ties to the past alongside the vague character of their accurate message.

When Pankaj left, the funeral parlor experienced a deep transformation that brought its energy down from explosive states to a determined calm sort of relief. Simply observing Mina from across the room, Prakash displayed signs that something was bothering him as his forehead creased deeply, reflecting his inner struggles. A soft light from the corridor entered the room, exposing bright shadows that danced across the shiny surface of the counter as both of them sank deeper into awareness about their situation.

"Our success will depend on showing him why this plan is valid, or else it will diminish Jayesh's reputation."

He declared this with deep disappointment in his tone.

The worry on his face revealed the potential path of his life, which caused a heavy sensation to build in his chest.

Through a composed stare, Mina looked at him without revealing the turmoil which raged inside her. She said this with confident certainty that suggested everything would be fine.

"We're not doing anything wrong. Our victory rests with Lord Shiva."

The directness of her words reverberated through the room along with the old spiritual prints that adorned the walls, which continued to observe their story. Each time the ancient wall clock ticked, the surroundings became more silent, thus heightening the intensity of their family bond. Prakash opened his palms to allow his fingers to let go of the counter's finish, and the tension dissipated like heat from what had only been moments ago fear-filled ground.

From his position at the darkest spot of the room, Jayesh observed each hesitation of his parents to accompany his private worry while he kept hidden. The mixed fragrance of incense carried from the preparation chambers entered through the doorway to symbolize their cultural heritage as well as an endless succession of traditional practices. The faraway normal noises from the outside world reminded their group of the delicate bond that tied them to the curious yet doubting members of their outside community. Prakash spoke his warning in a special tone, like revealing an important secret. **"Manorama was revered. Despite not wanting fame, she served her**

talents to the people."

The gentle shift from his spoken words brought out his hidden feelings. He could see his mother-in-law's smile linking real life with beyond as she waited for the light ceremony to start.

A gentle expression passed across Mina's face, giving a comforting feeling.

"We had good times with your mother, Mina, when she stayed with us. It's a shame she moved to India. Her kindness brought her both fondness and growth, which Prakash could feel through her words."

Their belief in God and their bond with the temple members brought them help and guidance.

The passing minutes were marked by both heartbeats and by the rising and falling of the light over their heads as they vowed their deep, mutual commitment. Their small family developed steady courage through each heartbeat as they promised to survive their family tradition without getting lost in what others think.

These words struck Prakash with emotion as he promised to shield his son Jayesh from harm.

"Our task is to protect what God gave us."

Jayesh felt his promise reach out and cover him like the protection of their family bond.

His parents strengthened their connection through their quiet discussions and shared memories that mixed their concerns with mutual convictions. They found a way to maintain peace between themselves, and Jayesh tried to follow their example. Through their calm dialogue, his parents shared wisdom that created inner strength for him.

Their family unity gave Prakash hope for the future as office lighting created shadows, and he relaxed his face to reveal his belief.

Chapter 6: "Geeta Sha's Last Message"

There was an ever-present murmur to the night, always undulating through the house where we lived. I shut myself up with books, with thousands of equations, with half-finished papers, trying to decipher meanings that were not so obvious. I was doing my homework in my bedroom.

There was the sound of wind blowing through the broken window and the sound of an old ceiling fan continuously rotating in my bedroom. Then, like a sudden flash in the blackness, the telephone rang.

It was the phone I received from my father. It was the phone of the body of Geeta Sha, and the ringing was a shiver. Finally, the phone rang! I hadn't had a call from a spirit for a couple of months. I picked up Geeta's phone eagerly.

"Hello?" My voice came out in a choked whisper. The static created an undertone sound and I could barely hear it because in my chest I could feel a rhythm pounding vigorously.

"Can you help me?" The voice began and was broken, far-off, and beaten. "My name is Geeta. I am in your father's funeral home."

When the phone rings, Jayesh always gets nervous and excited about what the new adventure Jayesh and Keyur will be on. The spirits always call on their own mobile phone.

"How can I help you?" said Jayesh. "Please tell me." Jayesh's voice came out with excitement.

The funny beep that sounded was a high-pitched sound, one that was quite shocking and caused a shiver to run down my spine. She started speaking in an Indian accent, and there was an increased passion in her voice.

"My children are in danger because my husband is hitting them. My husband's name is Bhavesh."

Every word crushed me over, difficult to breathe, as if there was a weight over me. Holding the phone tightly in my hand, I felt the cold plastic dig into the flesh of my palm.

Her children were in danger. Her voice cracked, becoming inaudible, and as I instinctively went to look for my voice, it refused to come out well.

"Why didn't you tell anyone?" It was a classical reaction that I could not hold back, and I said it, every word filled with shock.

"Don't tell me what I should have done!" She exclaimed violently. Her tone was vibrant and harsh, like tearing at flesh with a knife.

"Please can you go to the authorities," she said with some harshness in her voice. "I reside in Queensbury, North West region of London."

The line went silent, and I remained alone with the sound of the last words, and the pressure from the request that was made on me.

I couldn't get Geeta's words out of my head. Her voice was in sheer terror and anxiety. If it were true, every second spent in any other manner was in fact jeopardising the lives of Geeta's children.

I had to tell someone. I was waiting for Geeta's call eagerly. I looked through Geeta's phone for any information I could get, but even if I found something, what could I do? I had to wait for her to call again.

Geeta's words kept ringing in my mind like a movie replay that could not be switched off. All I could think of was Geeta's children, the last location that was provided, Queensbury, Northwest, London.

Again, I thought I had to tell someone. All of a sudden, I got up. I pushed my chair back. The time had come to tell my parents. I had to tell them there were kids' lives at risk.

As I rushed into the living area, the shadows crept and folded across it, and I moved with the fear that wrapped me like a fog.

My breath was so fast, shallow, but my mind was clearer. I was focused on what I had to do now.

Surrounded by the chill of Geeta's words, the icy whisper still rang through my skin.

Close by, my parents were talking in low, urgent tones. I didn't wait for them to look up.

"I got a call," I said, my voice just vibrating from the tremor of my resolve. "From Geeta."

I told them about the conversation in a torrent of words that spilled into one another, a plea for help and a desperate claim that her children were in danger from her husband, Bhavesh.

But I kept going, finding strength in my voice to give them everything, including the edge to her anger and her cold threat against our family.

The room was dense with the spirit's anger when I finally paused to draw breath.

Mina's head tipped, and her brow wrinkled softly. "That's odd," she whispered in a reassuring voice. "To my knowledge, I've never heard of a spirit getting angry like that."

Warm and with concern in them, her eyes met mine. "Are you alright, beta?"

The call was raw; and her question settled over me. Her steadiness was something strange, an odd comfort to the chaos running through me.

His focus was taut on his face, so Prakash was already on his feet. He clipped and was efficient.

"Let's call Pankaj. Tell him we've had contact."

Even with such unusual circumstances, the practical side of him surfaced. He thought of the business, of fulfilling the duty they'd been given.

I wanted to protest, but Mina started speaking again, this time her voice soft but strong.

"We have to move fast," she continued, looking from Prakash back to me. "If the spirit's saying is true, the kids are in danger."

Her words sounded urgent and unyielding in the air.

The ground closed in on me, the weight of the present hitting with a pressure I felt against my back.

Then all the urgency hit us and we all moved.

It had just been five minutes, and Prakash was already pacing the room with his phone in his hand, just about to call Pankaj and do something.

When he moved to stand beside him, Mina's fingers brushed my shoulder, and her touch anchored me to the storm.

I hardly heard what she said. My mind ran with all sorts of potentials, all of which I knew we didn't have much time.

What surprised me was they were so quick to help, and they jumped into accepting the spirit's threat as truth.

It burned a new determination in me, a resolve I did not know I had.

"I want to take the lead," I suddenly said, my voice growing stronger. "I can ask for more details. What else can I do?"

I needed to do something, anything to show that I was not just a messenger but an active participant in the solution.

I gave Mina a thoughtful look, and she nudged me as if thinking on my request.

She advised, "Ask them to share personal information," her words with the hard-learned knowledge of someone who knew much more than they told.

"Only the things that the family would know. So they will believe them."

That was the guidance I needed, and I clung to it as if to a lifeline.

Prakash's response was more pragmatic.

He agreed, not taking his eyes from the phone.

"But ensure it is something concrete. They won't listen unless we have evidence."

His practical nature went against that fear inside me, but I knew he was right.

If we were expecting to get out of this unscathed, we didn't have a plan.

Each person in the room confronted the magnitude of our task while the atmosphere grew heavier by the second.

My parents moved with the methodical organization of experienced professionals who had completed this operation numerous times before.

The unfamiliar environment helped me feel like a young child participating in adult matters before Mina spoke to me while I descended into confusion.

"Jayesh," she warned with a tone that showcased her concern throughout her composure.

"Besides your support we ask you to avoid all dangerous risks."

These words inserted a small doubt into my mind that teetered on the border between determination.

The dire need to intervene before everything was gone brought down my fears as swiftly as they arrived.

I straightened my posture to suppress the nervous movement that threatened to make me unstable.

Everything the night brought felt unreal and dreamlike, yet I kept myself focused and wide awake because I was determined to carry on.

As the discussion ended, the growing tension remained between us.

A strong grip surrounded us while the pressure from the air dwindled to nothingness.

The constant fear gripped my heart because I feared the phone would ring anytime to deliver another brutal request and peril.

The dangerous and unpredictable trail we were following did not scare me to stop trying.

The current air temperature made me inhale deeply as I let its coldness move through my body.

While the fear stayed close to me as an unpleasant visitor, it welcomed a new companion to its company, a sense of purpose, of conviction.

A fundamental shift was coming to my entire life which made itself evident to me.

Even though I knew the upcoming challenge would not allow any backout opportunities, I prepared myself for what lay in front.

Chapter 6: "Geeta Sha's Last Message" - Part Two

I was seated in the dark at home and waited. Beside a photo lay the phone on the table. Each time I looked, there was another call that was unanswered, and it seemed to shine like something alive, like a heart.

On the third attempt, I took it and said, "Hello." My voice seemed to emanate from a place deep within me that was far stronger than I was right now.

At first, it was just occasional pops and cracks on the line. "What are your kids' names?" I questioned, and thus I got a stuttering response.

The woman's voice was cracked and filled with anger as she responded back to me.

I tightened my grip on the phone as she went on speaking to me. Shalesh was the boy, and the girl was named Pinky.

"Geeta, I need some private information that only you and Bhavesh would know."

Geeta said, "Why are you wasting time?" she said angrily.

Jayesh said, "I am only 13 years old. I will have to convince them that I am not talking rubbish."

Geeta's voice changed into a kind tone. "I am sorry, my daughter had a birthmark. An unfortunate incident that happened in the past."

Her voice cut like glass through the static. The breath left my chest. The details, the urgency. It felt like she stood at the side of me inside the room, her strength uncompromising.

"They should be told about it openly and informed that Pinky has a birthmark on her head, the back of the left ear particularly.

I was once careless when dealing with Shalesh and ended up dropping him off a rocking chair when he was just a baby.

That only my husband Bhavesh and I know, not even my two elder sisters or anyone else."

I put the phone down to arm's length, but its din penetrated deeper into the room like her voice. There was no escaping it.

"The final thing that I need you to do," said Geeta, "is that Bhavesh needs to be reported to the police, that he is physically and mentally assaulting the kids."

The line crackled with the tones of her raised voice, then silence came back, and with it, phrases poured in.

The children were in danger. These words she said at length, speaking louder and in a stronger voice as if each time that she repeated the words, she was asserting her dominance over him.

"Do you understand me? You have to help them."

The sound of the buzzing line was ringing in my ear. The words lodged like hooks, in the same way like stones.

This was filled with a tangible presence of the woman.

What she uttered left me; what she wanted me to do sent my head spinning.

Tell the police.

This means that it would be able to say what no one else is able to say under any given circumstances or condition.

Her voice rose in volume of pitch as well as of agony and despair. Then it stopped.

Silence arrived as black ink on white paper, and I was standing there holding the phone with such tight grip that I could feel its heartbeat which was one with mine.

I dropped the phone onto the table and leaned against the wall.

Her vocal performance held a chilling nature as the viewer felt the rawness of the sound.

She would not let go of me until I complied or until I told whatever she wanted to make known.

My fingers tightened. It became a bit difficult for me to breathe, and the results were very shallow breaths.

It did not fade, this determination, this fear.

They had to know, the police.

It took me to be the one to break the news.

Pankaj was in front of me all of a sudden, his features distorted by fear.

My father had called Pankaj for him to witness for himself how I used my gifts.

Pankaj did not utter a word.

After I relayed what Geeta was saying to my mum and dad, "We must go to Queensbury right now," my dad said. "There is no time to lose."

My dad said, "I will call the police from the car. Let's go quickly."

We were all about to get in the car when my mum Mina said, "Please, can I come as well?"

"OK," my dad said. "Get in quickly."

When my mum came along, it made me feel at ease. Now I felt nothing could harm me.

Pankaj was riding in the front of the car sitting next to my dad.

"Are you sure about this, Jayesh?" Pankaj said.

I nodded, too afraid to face the truth rather than to be wrong.

It was a quiet street. We drove up to Geeta's house in Queensbury.

We could see two officers stood waiting outside the house.

We could see two children in the back of the police car.

My father didn't hesitate. He ran straight to the officers and spoke in a low voice.

"Officer, I am Prakash. I was the one who rang you. Is Bhavesh here? Did you get here in time?"

The officer nodded and pointed to the front of the house. He kept the other hand on his belt and said, "Don't worry, the children are safe."

I was stunned by the sight of Shalesh and Pinky, so small, so still.

My father's voice grew louder.

"Officer, if Bhavesh asks you how I know Geeta and Bhavesh's family, please tell him I am from Prakash Funeral Parlour.

I am looking after the funeral preparations for his late wife.

And if Bhavesh asks for any proof of how I know his children, please tell him I know about the birthmark Pinky has behind her left ear, and how Geeta accidentally dropped Shalesh from the rocking chair when Shalesh was young."

The officer looked at Prakash strangely.

"OK," he said.

Then another officer approached and said, "Are you Prakash?"

"Yes," my dad said.

"I am the officer you were speaking to on the phone. We are speaking to Bhavesh in the house."

Just then, the door burst open. Bhavesh appeared, frantic and wild-eyed.

"Please listen to me, officers, for a moment!! Please!!" His voice cracked with desperation.

"You've got this all wrong, officers.

The person beating the kids has been Geeta.

Geeta has been diagnosed with schizophrenia. If she forgets to take her medication, she lies and gets very aggressive."

But I wanted to run to him and tell him it was not true. I heard her voice; I felt her presence. But the weight of his words belayed me.

He expected the officers to have dismissed this frantic man.

Bhavesh insisted that it was Geeta that they should be worried about.

"Not me. Not the children."

The silence was long and heavy.

The officers glanced at each other.

They glanced at the kids in the car, their bruised and fragile arms.

One officer told them, "You should have called the hospital and told them about it."

My mother gripped her hand on mine.

I heard the words of the woman, her commanding insistence, her fierce desperation.

Then, a doctor arrived, and again the scene changed.

The voices of the officers were a low murmur that I tried to make out.

Bhavesh's account was confirmed by Geeta's psychiatrist, they said.

Her condition. Her violence.

The officers released Bhavesh.

I saw the children fly towards his side, hugging him with relief.

Bhavesh kissed both kids.

"Don't worry. I am here," said Bhavesh.

I couldn't believe what was happening.

Bhavesh walked away with the children.

I was in a daze.

What had just happened?

We had come all this way for what, to be made fools of?

"How did Geeta die?" asked Prakash, his tone sharp, with his shoulders trembling.

Bhavesh held the children close.

Bhavesh said, "Geeta took an overdose of her medication."

Just then Bhavesh said angrily, "How do you know about all this, Prakash?"

Bhavesh looked at Prakash like he was in intense thought.

"Can we speak in private, Bhavesh?" Prakash asked.

"Sure. Come in my house."

Mina, Prakash, Jayesh, and Pankaj went into his house.

Geeta's house was very nicely decorated.

We went into the living room.

"Please have a seat. I will be back in a minute. I want to give the children a bite to eat."

"Shall I give you a hand?" Mina said.

"No, it's OK. I will do it. Please give me a few minutes."

"Take your time."

Bhavesh took his children into the kitchen and gave them something to eat and put the television on for them.

When Bhavesh came into the living room, he sat down and said, "Your funeral parlour is looking after Geeta's funeral preparations, am I right?"

"Yes," said Prakash.

"I want to know, how did you know about any of this?"

Prakash told Bhavesh about Jayesh's gift and how he can speak to the spirits through the mobile phone of the deceased.

He told him what happened when Geeta communicated with Jayesh and what she had said, that Bhavesh was abusing the children.

Jayesh asked her for some personal information only he and Geeta would know.

Geeta told Jayesh about the birthmark behind Pinky's left ear and how Geeta accidentally dropped Shalesh from the rocking chair when he was very young.

Bhavesh looked at them in amazement.

"There is no way you would have known this."

"But I don't understand," said Prakash, "why did she lie to us?"

"It's her illness," said Bhavesh. "She always lied. Her schizophrenia was getting worse.

It was her illness that made her do these things. She was getting more and more violent.

I thought if the doctors adjusted her medication, she would be able to control her violence.

She was once a beautiful and loving person."

"I have heard of your gift, Jayesh. I know you have helped quite a few people," said Bhavesh.

"I am sorry to have caused you so much trouble," said Jayesh.

"Please don't say sorry, Jayesh. It's not your fault."

"Let's go now," said Mina. "We don't want to waste any more of your time. Your kids need you."

They all got up and left Bhavesh's house.

In the car drive home, I could see mum had so much to say.

"Why would she lie? I have never known of spirits to lie," said Mina.

I sat down and leaned my head against the back of the car seat.

It was not how things were planned to be or how most people expected them to be in this match.

Even when the children were safe, I could not escape the feeling of being pursued by Geeta.

This was not the end. I was certain of it.

I couldn't get rid of some parts of the sad and desperate words that came out of Geeta's mouth.

My mother made masala chai after returning.

Her hands were shaking a little as she gave me the tea.

"The cup of hot tea, drink!" she said. "It will calm your nerves. Please, Pankaj bhai, drink it while it's hot, please."

But there wasn't anything I could do that would calm my nerves at this moment.

Pankaj had walked off, without saying what anyone could not imagine was worse than his not uttering a word.

My father went back to his room, shutting the door against queries, against any inkling of this chaos.

I was left physically alone with the responsibilities for what had occurred and the doubts about what was real.

That night I couldn't sleep.

The ceiling fan above my bed was slowly rotating, and as the light fell upon the walls, it flickered, shaking weakly.

At three in the morning, I suddenly woke with my legs tangled in the bed sheets.

I got out of bed and went to the window.

There were no people around on the street, and the only thing that illuminated the darkness was a dim light coming from the street lamps.

Just then, I thought I saw something out of the ordinary on the other side of the street.

I blinked, and it was gone.

I thought I saw an outline of a lady standing and staring at me.

Geeta's spirit was in my head.

Chapter 7: "Dealing with Geeta the Aggressive Spirit"

As we sat around the breakfast table in the morning, I asked my mum for a cup of masala tea. Mina looked at Jayesh and said, "Did you sleep okay, son? Because you look tired."

"I couldn't get Geeta's voice out of my head," said Jayesh.

"I know, my love. I couldn't sleep too last night," said Mina. "But I do think we should attend Geeta's funeral, to give support to Bhavesh and his children."

"Yes, I think we should," said Prakash. "I think we should take Pankaj with us."

"Why?" said Mina.

"Because we need him on our side until he writes the article."

"I suppose you are right," said Mina.

Dad called Pankaj and asked him if he wanted to come with us. Pankaj accepted our invite.

My father went down to the funeral parlour, and his staff put Geeta's coffin in the hearse. The driver and the funeral celebrant , the person who looks after the funeral , left in the hearse.

We picked up Pankaj on the way to Bhavesh's house.

When we got to Bhavesh's house, my dad went up to Bhavesh, shook his hand, and gave him a hug.

It was a very sombre funeral.

After the funeral, we said our goodbyes to Bhavesh and his kids and got in our car to go home.

On our way home, I could see Pankaj was still stunned about what he had witnessed the other day when he came with us to tell Bhavesh about what Geeta's spirit said to us.

Pankaj was in deep thought.

Jayesh was of two minds, relieved that the children were happy and still very angry that Geeta had lied to him.

At least, Jayesh thought, when Pankaj writes his article, he won't poke fun at Jayesh.

Every stoplight meant the time stopped, the wait elongated as if it lasted for many hours.

My father's usual way of sitting quietly, that meant he was deep in thought, suddenly froze into a kind of heavy stillness, and he sat staring straight at the road in front of him, a thousand miles away into a world and a fight I could only half fathom.

Pankaj was sitting right next to me, looking as shocked as he was the other day.

I could see and feel the tension in him as though the adrenaline rushing through his veins wished to leap out of his body.

It was indecisive as to whether I should console him or express amazement at the fact. My head was filled with confusion and fear.

All fatigue ensued at last, and the car drew up to our small house as the evening descended heavy as a damp towel.

I felt relaxed when my house came in sight.

The home with so many fantastic memories.

Driving up to my house brought a sense of comfort and feeling of safety.

We could feel the tone of the surrenders , so close we were to our reality of a family funeral parlour next door.

Pankaj remained in the car for a few seconds before following us, his lips clamped shut and his face indicating he was preparing for another fight , this time against forces he could not see.

Mina was standing in the living room with her arms folded across her chest, and her posture was somewhat vulnerable.

She was a brilliant woman, and she looked somewhat downcast.

Her eyes had lost their sparkle as she looked towards Prakash.

She said, "I think we need to contact Geeta. We have to speak to her, and we need her to ask her why she lied."

"You are right," said Prakash.

Without delay, he picked up Geeta's mobile phone from the table.

His steps were well measured, unhesitant.

He handed it to me with such a deadly serious demeanor that it reverberated in my arteries.

It became an enclosed space and bare, too: an allegory of a room that had been converted into a confessional chamber where secrets could not hide. Pankaj stood motionless at the door of Jayesh's house; a man detached in his people's territory. He eyeballed them with a shocked expression painted all over his face. Each time our hands touched our knees, as we stood enclosed in the circle of the low-hung light, which seemed to be a plea a call to the slumbering forces of the night, to answer the call.

That is a glimpse of the everyday life: holding the phone, its metal frame being cold with my palm that helps me remain anchored to reality in the midst of what feels like a spinning out of control. I could sense the pounding hearts and unsaid sparks between us and the secrets and anticipation that filled our room like the air we breathed.

My hands shook when I picked up the phone and everything else turned hazy in memory of panic. As I faced the incoming event I felt immense pressure build up combined with hard beats matching the planned disaster. Every gaze in the room hung onto me as people waited expectantly like the tension before an electric storm.

I hit the call button with quivering breathing. No sound seemed to exist except my own thoughts as the universe joined me in anticipation of what was about to happen. The loud crackling noise coming from the speaker shattered the building anxiety like shattered glass. "Why did you do that?" The speaker made its way into the room with a loud and angry tone. "You've tarnished my name! I hate Bhavesh! The result would have been his imprisonment because of your disobedience he is going to get away with it why didn't you do what I said!!" said Geeta angrily.

I recognized the truth at once as if someone had slapped me in the face. Speaking to Geeta all that was in my mind was why did she lie and the poor children it could have turned out absolutely horrible for them. A flood of strong emotions dashed through me when I shut my eyes. "Why did you lie to me?" Surprise pushed me to defend myself. "Your children would have entered foster care due to your fabrication."

The environment became tense as if the wall panels had moved in their positions to listen to our discussion. Alarm accelerated my heart when Geeta transformed from her voice into an evil presence. The faint silhouette became more defined there while a ghostly face took shape revealing its bitterful expression that caused my spine to shiver. My body jerked away from the presence because a sudden urge to flee flooded through me.

"Go away and leave us alone!" Mina spoke with motherly determination to face down our rising terror. The woman extended her powerful figure to block the spectral presence from the room. Geeta's chilling laughter erased Mina's confidence in one frozen moment. Mina held Jayesh's hand to protect him. Mina couldn't believe what she was seeing. She was concerned about Jayesh.

The shock paralyzed Pankaj in his place as marks formed on his bare forehead. He began to develop shock at the abnormal situation we entered. "What the hell is going on?" He spoke in shock with broken words to seek clarity among the madness.

The ghostly presence of Geeta disturbed us as it shifted in the darkness reminding us that we depend on life and death to survive our existential shock. My mind could not understand who created this terror situation.

Our tension grew high as we faced the horrifying scene still unfolding before us. Despite the feeling of momentum in the room it brought us nothing but bad prospects and a mix of fear and excitement confused our understanding.

The sudden light flicker added to our sense of endangerment and made us face the cruel path that threatened our lives. Our inevitable change started when we faced a decisive point that brought together our fear and defiance before the damage of our actions became clear.

Tension filled the air as Mina frantically typed away at the screen of her phone, the only link, the only outlet of power to combat the growing uncertainty enveloping us. Each ring was heavy with a prayer for forgiveness and the saving of our souls, and my mother's face showed me a courage that I needed to embrace while the storm of sorrow entered our home uninvited.

"Please hurry," she said softly into the receiver, her voice shaking. Jayesh gave a look of surprise to his mother. Mina clasped Jayesh's hand and said in a soft voice, "Your grandmother is here from India. She took a flight yesterday; she is on her way here." Mina's mother Manorama has had the gift to speak to spirits since she was a child, like Jayesh. When Mina spoke to her mother Manorama on the phone two days ago, Manorama was worried. She told Mina, "Don't worry, I will get the next flight."

A few minutes later, a knock at the door brought a wave of hope to all of us. My spirit seemed to leap at the sight of her; Manorama was one of those people whose aura began even before one could spot charm in her looks. Manorama looked so elegant and calm it made all my fears completely go away. I felt a sense of relief. For this, I can thank my lucky stars that I had a steady face to look upon after the commotion I saw to my horror and relief.

"Dadi," I whispered the title out loud, not believing that I am saying it but happy all the same.

She, now in her early sixties silver headed advanced gracefully into the living room leaning slightly on the frame of the door. It felt as if she was loaded with generations of experience; with each step a spirit came alive. Having a calm air was the last thing that could be expected from her given the raging storm outside; when Manorama walked in the room it had a calming effect on everyone in the room.

"Jayesh," she said firmly, it was evident that the kind of rationality the Hardin needed was something she was willing to deliver with an iron will. "This would mean that the person needs to undergo a ritual in order to remove her from one's life." Manorama leaped into action with a voice of determination she said quickly "everyone we have to do the ritual Puja very quickly there is no time to waste." When she started preparing for puja amidst the surrounded furniture in the living room there was a feeling of togetherness which was preparing itself for a mobilization that would support her determination.

I called Keyur and my voice was so low because the energy level in the hall was high. Keyur was shocked at what he was witnessing. Outside I shivered, as though the boundary between this earth and the other worlds was getting lower.

Shivani sat on the corner and then suddenly she started crying, deeply; crying as if there was no one else present in the vicinity. "Do not be frightened, my child," Manorama said to her grandchild, positioning herself closer to her as a source of comfort, a reassuring mother. I remember some kind words were: "I won't let anyone hurt you."

Immediately and nonchalantly, Manorama quickly lit a small candle to the Hindu deity and with grace, she began to chant some verses from the holy book. It appeared that the room was personalized and breathed history and still does, so even feeling our aloneness in bitterness wasn't that terrible. Manorama started to speak to the angry spirit of Geeta and her words shook the air around us.

"What do you want to do, see how close you can get to sending me back?" A chilling echo of disdain rang out of her laughter. Her presence was a malevolent fog infiltrating our fragile sanctuary, the moment was visceral. My heart was racing and I clenched the phone tighter, my instincts telling me to leave.

Manorama's command shattered the tension. "Leave this house and these lives of this family." The ghost's taunts were a shallow echo compared to the faith that filled her voice. "No way! I begin to think Geeta is going to torture us."

Then the candle flared like a tempest caught in opposing forces, trying to reach for somewhere away from those hands, but Manorama was resolute, her brow determined. With no dawdling, she lit the candle fully, the flame flickering bright in the shadows, shining on the faces surrounding her.

She quickly took out the phone's battery and threw it into the fire that was blazing away. Geeta's form dissolved, and a fading echo of something once powerful, and she cut through the air with a piercing scream. The final specter of Geeta disappeared into lingering tension before the flames settled and danced wildly, their last dance done.

The last embers of Geeta faded from our living room and was instantly followed by a deep, deafening silence. Manorama announced, her voice a note of finality that was so fragile a relief. Shadows of uncertainty, lingered, never really disappearing like smoke clinging to our shoulders.

Grounding urged himself back to the real world as Prakash shook his head slowly, but the anxiety didn't fade. His face was still drawn tight. "We have to stop this now. What if it happens again?" The father's instinct flared up, his words were firm, a testament to what we had just been through.

Manorama gave me a steady gaze and said, "Your son has a gift." "He also can lend a great hand to a lot of disturbed souls and families." Her tone was consoled, yet her acceptance meant I had some potential of being grounded in the moment, and Pankaj stood still and rooted, disbelief frozen on his face, a witness to an unexplainable reality.

Silence, and the strange one, enveloped us all, the result of a mix of relief and lingering dread as we tried to process what we had found. Geeta's voice was silenced, but the ghostly traces of our encounter left sorer prints in our lives, etched with the fragility of the world we inhabited and the weight of our load in the cycle of life that was wrought with dark and light.

Chapter 8: "The Price of Fame"

A couple of weeks went by after the horrifying moment when Geeta's spirit manifested in front of our eyes. My grandmother was going to stay with us for a few weeks.

Jayesh came down from his bedroom in his school uniform and sat down for breakfast. Manorama had made a special breakfast. My grandmother was a fantastic cook.

My dad sat next to me and said, "Are you okay, son?"

"Yes," I said.

"Listen, son, Pankaj's article comes out today, so maybe your friends and teachers may have read the article."

"Don't worry. I have seen the article. Pankaj promised me I could see it before it went to press. It's a great article."

Through the colorful and noisy school hallways, I walked as though trapped in a jail of secrets that lingered at my back like spirits. My classmates avoided eye contact with me while laughing strangely because most people had read Pankaj's newspaper article before I did.

Clans of students formed tight groups to whisper animatedly as they focused their quick glances at me. The negative and admiring whispers flowed toward me like a sharp knife slicing into my flesh. They whispered, "Have you seen the article?" with strong interest in their voices.

Those gathered in my vicinity could sense my unease because their words about the article floated through the air with an unpleasant sweet fragrance.

Backpacks and arms bumped against me while I walked, yet my heart pumped wildly against the wall of discomfort in my chest. I wanted to vanish among rows of lockers and attach myself to every poster on the walls.

Mr. Spencer stepped aside to let me approach the classroom corner and stood with his hands together while watching me guardedly.

"How are you?" said Mr. Spencer, who is my form teacher.

"I read the article, Jayesh. It was very interesting." He looked at me through his piercing gaze, but his warmth shined like the sun breaking through heavy clouds.

His glance showed me that he approved of me and at the same time pushed me down. At that second, I wanted to give back to him with genuine confidence, but my self-doubt held me down.

"Thank you, Mr. Spencer, sir," I spoke with a faint hesitation as students glanced at us while showing different facial expressions.

I was surprised by the reactions of everyone at school. I thought I was going to be a mockery at school with kids shouting out funny jokes at my expense. But I could sense a feeling of mystery in people's eyes when they looked at me.

The silence around me didn't end until my perception of time began to slow, and I felt them all as they murmured and pressed on me.

The teacher stepped near me while speaking with intensity.

"Understanding this gift requires patience. The subject goes beyond printed news, Jayesh. Your talent transforms into value through action."

Just then I saw Keyur. He came towards me through the groups of students in the corridor.

Keyur walked with a spring in his step, like he was in with the most popular boy in the school.

"Hi Jayesh, have you read the article? It's made you look like you are a Marvel superhero.

I am going to name you Captain Spirit Talker and get you a superhero costume with your name on it," Keyur said and had a great big smile on his face.

"People are looking at me differently," I said.

"They are looking at you with envy, and it's better than how they looked at you before, Jayesh.

They used to call you rude names behind your back," said Keyur with a small laugh.

Mr. Spencer indicated the exit with a movement of his hand to invite me to leave. The other students' gazes followed me as I left the classroom, making me think about all the different ways they viewed my gift.

The distance from those I could have regarded as friends was as heavy as a physical burden, and that was the first time I experienced the weight of fame, not being proud of what I could do, or in my gift, when it turned into loneliness and the loss of people I could turn to.

Relationships became impersonal and distant.

Entering Mr. Spencer's room in an environment containing fluorescent lights felt like walking in a judge's chamber. There were posters of Albert Einstein with famous quotes he had said and maps of different countries.

Mr. Spencer sat behind a big wooden desk to infuse everyone who sat in front of him with icy fear.

Mr. Spencer faced me; the look in his eyes was authoritative, but the man gave off the aura of a protective figure.

"Jayesh, these papers tell me that your schoolwork is not too good anymore. You should try more and better. Jayesh do not think this article and your gifts will give you special treatment."

Every phrase that escaped his mouth was like the assembling of a concrete wall when the words themselves were his concrete.

"You must tell your parents to come to parents evening today. I have to instruct your mum and dad to oversee your work or instructions that you are given."

I felt my insides twist.

"I am trying my best, Mr. Spencer. As you read in the paper, I have had a lot on my mind lately, sir," I said, barely able to speak the words through the rage building up inside me.

How could I tell my teacher that I have been having terrible nightmares at night, so I haven't had a good night's sleep in weeks?

"It's not just about your gift," he continued, this time speaking more harshly, his voice severing the building mist that clouded my mind.

"It is always a good idea to seek the right combination of both the home and the workplace. This is about your future."

Mr. Spencer's eyes were fixed on me. I could see he wanted me to explode with anger so he could have something more to complain to my parents about over parents evening, but I remained calm.

Time, as marked by the buzzing fluorescent light above, started ticking, and the teacher adjusted himself.

"Oh, you are not the sum of these headlines, Jayesh. Do not let your talents and what you can do go to waste."

As I nodded, the feeling of dread grew even stronger.

I came out of his office with that sinking feeling in my throat and a scream that was dying to get out.

I was just a kid for whom being simply a part of a group was enough, who never dreamed of a light being shone upon the dark part of my life.

When Jayesh's mum and dad came back home from the parents evening at Jayesh's school later in the evening, the silence closed around me like a scaly skin of a dead animal.

I was expecting my father to scold me, with each of the steps he took producing a new groan from the floor.

He sat at the marred dining table, fiddling with the grooves on the tabletop as the aroma of Mina's cooking enveloped the air, bringing solace, yet something more, a feeling of impending dread.

She fixed her mouth into a disapproving line; from the neighboring room, I could hear the television humming, a retreat from reality, although it was not effective in dispelling my restlessness.

Prakash straightened up, his serious look intensified and he was more rigid than usual.

"Jayesh, look, your education is far more valuable than the gift you have.

Jayesh, life isn't easy out in the real world.

Education is what will get you to university and get a great job," he continued his speech.

These words were like hot filling the antenna of my mind.

My father kept on talking to me in an angry voice.

"Jayesh, it's very hard out there to get a job without a university degree.

I'm not going to be here forever working in my funeral parlour, Jayesh."

I erupted, and the aggression came pouring out like a spigot.

"It is not my fault that I was blessed with this talent, and I never wished to work here at your undertakers."

"Don't talk silly. I expect you to become more proactive."

The tension was palpable when Prakash said this, and the disappointment seemed to radiate off him, causing an electric current of conflict.

My heart pounded dangerously in my chest; I thrust my chair back, and it clattered against the floor.

My mother ran in the room and said, "Come on everyone, please calm down!"

There was an awkward silence in the room.

"Come on, Jayesh, pick up your chair and sit down and eat your dinner," said my mum.

Prakash gave me an angry look and was about to speak, and Mina said to him, "Please don't say another word, Prakash.

This boy has been through things that no other child his age has gone through, and he has seen things that would even make a grown adult quake in his boots.

I am only worried about you, son," said Prakash.

"All I want is for you not to fall behind in your studies," said Prakash.

I was still fuming in my mind.

I had to get out of there before I said something I would regret.

I went upstairs to my room and, closing the door to my room upstairs, I fell on the bed, wrapping the smell of my room around me to protect me from exploding inside.

I started to ask myself how I was to deal with expectations and gifts and all that in between when everything around seemed to be falling on me.

That night, I saw myself in the clutches of a dark unknown.

In the darkness of dreams, I set out on a trip with Geeta's spirit, damnation hungry and gnashing her eyes for more.

Every scream that she let out seemed to vibrate in the very core of my brain, connected to a very real horror, and every time I opened my eyes to the morning dawn, the memory of her anger came with me.

It was only a glimmer when at last it seeped between the slats of the curtain as I loathed the light.

The moment I woke up, I saw my room as it was, but the reality was twisted by all that I was experiencing in my nightmares.

Exhaustion followed me like a cloak suffocating me as I forced myself to sit up from the entangled bedclothes and regretted that it wasn't a nightmare I could scrub away.

The day lay in front of me like a concrete, tangible thing, but the reality around them was distorted.

My clumsy walk led me to the funeral parlor, and with every pace I took, echoes of my dreams followed me.

The processes prior to the arrival of the unclaimed body were undertaken in an unchanging cadence triggered by the low vibration of motion that ran through the familiar halls.

Then I saw my parents just when a car was approaching the gate, its arrival darkening the spirit of the day.

Prakash and Mina glanced at each other knowingly.

The grim reality was, this was our reality, a reminder of our duties in our world, in our home, for our family.

The dead body was carried in and was covered by a white sheet that respected the occasion.

A certain tension of strickeness in the atmosphere of the house and whispers surrounded the continuous activity of the staff members.

But there too was hidden an undertow of sadness, a respect for those people who had been through the bitterness of having lost everything.

I knew that this dead body must have a phone which I may have to contact his spirit with.

When Prakash lifted the sheet, there was a man, homeless, with skin stretched on his bones, the thin frame with lines on the face saying the story of hunger.

There was a familiar pinch at the back of my neck.

I looked away at the cell phone tucked deep in his pocket, a small item full of potential of bridging the gap between life for some and death for others.

"Jayesh, Jayesh," my dad said twice, bringing me back from a deep daydream.

"What are you thinking about, son? Are you okay?"

Prakash stepped in Jayesh's bedroom and handed the phone to Jayesh.

"It's the phone of the body that just arrived," my dad said.

My fingers quivered when my dad put the cold phone in my hand.

A chill ran down my spine.

I stared at the phone thinking I don't want this phone. I do not need this phone at this vulnerable state I am in.

But I took it, waiting for it to ring and give me instructions on what he needs me to do.

Mina could see Jayesh was nervous to answer the phone to speak to the dead body's spirit.

Mina said, "Are you okay, Jayesh? What's wrong, Jayesh? Please speak to me."

Jayesh looked his mum in the eyes and started to cry.

Mina held Jayesh in her arms.

"What's wrong Jayesh?" Mina had a worried look about her.

"Please talk to me, Jayesh."

Nevertheless, that admission seemed empowering because there is nothing quite like having the truth hanging in the air between two people.

In the company of my mother, I felt calm, safe, and protected.

She put her arms around me and said, "Do not worry, my dear child, I am always here for you," she said softly, her words filled with love and empathy.

A burst of bright energy entered the room when Keyur walked through the door just as a winter sun would bring light to daylight.

Keyur offered to play PlayStation, and his youthful tone and playful manner helped me relax throughout this moment.

My friendship connected to my familiar world, the world I knew.

Me and Keyur played and laughed. It felt like we hadn't had a normal evening like this in years.

Manorama entered my room shortly afterwards, which brought a calming influence to soothe the shaken state of my disposition.

"Your fear is evident to me right now, Jayesh," she stated directly in her soft melodic tone.

"The weight of these challenges exceeds what any children your age could handle.

"But you possess a unique ability to offer assistance to the people in our world and the spirit realm.

"Jayesh, I need to help you to control your emotional state of mind and help you with the fear you are feeling.

"Your mother, father, and Keyur, together with you, I will teach all of you how to help you use the gift you possess."

A discerning look from her eyes brought peace to my unsettled state.

"The spirits can't hurt you. Don't worry about that.

"You can resolve angry spirits by disconnecting the phone or asserting clearly that they should not speak to you like that.

"I am trying to help you."

A wave of understanding emerged inside me when I paid attention to her words because the earlier tension became nonexistent.

"Understand when to answer calls by having your parent join you or by having either of them present," she advised, guiding me through my mental storm.

I listened to her words with deep intent while the family network embraced me like a desert tuning into the wetness of rain-bearing winds.

The rhythm of my heart brought reassuring promises of bravery during the challenging times that would approach.

My gift required teamwork since it linked our souls beyond existence and non-existence.

Jayesh came down in the morning to the kitchen for breakfast. He saw his mum and dad were in deep thought. "Mum, can Keyur come home after school today to play PlayStation today?" My dad said, "What about your homework?" "I will do it when Keyur goes home; he is only coming for a couple of hours," I said. Jayesh's dad gave him an angry look. "No homework first, Jayesh, then you can play your PlayStation all you want."

Shivani gave Jayesh a sarcastic smile. Prakash got up and went down to his funeral parlour. "What's wrong with dad?" asked Jayesh. "Your dad is getting lots of calls from people asking if you can contact their dead relatives, and we are getting calls from so many newspapers, and we had a call from a few Asian TV channels. He thinks life will change for all of us," she explained. "Come on, Jayesh, you better get to school. I am making Mutter Paneer and parathas today."

"Fantastic," said Jayesh. "Ask Keyur to come home for dinner, tell him to do his homework here, I will give his mother a call in a while."

On the way to school, Jayesh told Keyur about all the calls his dad had received from the press and the Asian TV channels. "Woh," said Keyur, "your family is going to be really famous. Can I have your autograph now before you get too famous?" Keyur said jokingly.

At school, Jayesh and Keyur met three of their other friends outside the school gate: Kevin Mason, Paul Viddler, and Arshad Shah. "Hi everyone," but they all looked quite upset. "What's wrong?" said Jayesh. Kevin said, "Arshad's uncle passed away in Pakistan."

"So sorry to hear that, Arshad," we all gave him a hug. "What happened, was he ill?" I asked. "Jayesh, my dad wanted to speak to you. If it's okay, he said he will come at lunchtime to see you." "Sure," I said in my head, knowing what he was going to ask.

In school, Jayesh saw Mr. Spencer on the playground. Mr. Spencer walked up to Jayesh. "Hello, Jayesh. How are you getting on?" asked Mr. Spencer.

"Very well, Sir, thank you," answered Jayesh.

"The test we had in class a couple of days ago, you did very well. You got 93%. That talk I had with your mum and dad on parents' evening did a lot of good," said Mr. Spencer. "Well done and keep it up."

Mr. Spencer walked away and left Jayesh. I was trying hard, but I had lots of things on my mind. Jayesh wanted to shout it out at the top of his voice. The 5 lessons Jayesh had before lunch went very slowly. Jayesh couldn't think properly because he kept thinking about what Mr. Shah was going to say at lunchtime.

At lunchtime, Jayesh, Arshad, Keyur, and Kevin went outside the school gates to meet Mr. Shah, Arshad's dad. Mr. Shah was a tall, slim gentleman. He was a very kind person. Mr. Shah and my dad were very good friends. I have known Mr. Shah since I was 5 years old.

"Hello, boys," said Mr. Shah. "How are all of you?"

"Boys, I need to speak to Jayesh in private. Please give me a few minutes," he said. "Here, I have got you all some samosas your Auntie has made." Everyone's eyes lit up. Mrs. Shah's samosas were legendary.

"Let's talk in the car," Mr. Shah said. We got in the car, and Mr. Shah told me to eat my samosa. Mr. Shah began to speak about his brother in Pakistan.

"Jayesh, you know my brother, his name is Mustafa." "Yes," I said. "We met him when we came for a visit from Pakistan and had dinner at our house." "Yes, that's him. How can I help you, uncle?"

"Jayesh, my brother passed away yesterday. He died in his sleep. I wonder, son, would you be able to contact him? I have his mobile phone," he said.

"Uncle, I can only contact spirits from my father's funeral parlour, and they only contact me if something is troubling them."

"Please, Jayesh, can you just have a go, please?" he said, with a tear in his eye.

"Sure, uncle, but I have never spoken to a spirit from outside my father's funeral parlour." I couldn't say no to him because Mr. Shah was like a father to me.

Mr. Shah gave me his brother's phone. My friend was coming to the UK last night, so I asked him to bring Mustafa's phone for me. I held his phone, and the hairs on the back of my neck stood with excitement. Could I speak to a spirit from a different country?

I switched on the phone and said, "Hello, hello," but there was no answer. "Hello, hello," I said again, but again, no answer.

"Sorry, uncle, he is not there. As I said, uncle, I have only spoken to spirits inside my dad's funeral parlour."

Mr. Shah was very upset. "Do you think his death was suspicious?" I asked.

"No, I don't," said Mr. Shah. "I just wanted to say goodbye or something."

"And they only speak to me if their soul is not at peace," I said.

"Thank you for trying, Jayesh." I got out of the car and met up with my friends.

After school, Jayesh and Keyur went home. When they got to Jayesh's house, Prakash, Jayesh's dad, and Mina were sitting in the kitchen. Prakash was on the phone talking angrily to a reporter. "No, you can't come to my funeral parlour for an interview," said Prakash. "I don't care how much money you can pay me," Prakash slammed the phone down. "It's been relentless, these phone calls," said Prakash to Mina. "I have had enough."

"Look, Prakash, the public is interested in these kinds of stories," said Mina.

"I know, I would be," said Mina.

Jayesh hinted to Keyur, "Let's go to my room." They both went to Jayesh's room when Prakash shouted out,

"Do your homework first before you play on the PlayStation."

"Okay," said Jayesh. Keyur asked, "What is your dad so angry about?"

"The media and the press are hounding my dad for interviews," Jayesh explained. "Well, what do you expect, Jayesh? It must be one of the most interesting subjects to read about."

They went down for dinner. The smell in the house was unbelievable. Mina put a big pot of Mutter Paneer on the table with hot parathas.

Jayesh said over dinner to his mum, "How did Dadi Ma and Masi deal with their gift when they were young?"

"It was very hard," Mina replied. "If people found out that someone in your family had a gift where you could talk to spirits, people would think we were doing black magic. We had to keep it very quiet. No one could ever find out. In India, where we grew up, it was a very religious country, and there were a lot of fake, bogus holy men. My father, your grandfather Jayesh, wasn't religious at all. He used to tell us, 'Don't let religion control your life.' My dad tried to stop my mother and sister from using their gifts."

"The dinner was absolutely fantastic, Auntie. Thank you," said Keyur.

"You don't have to say thank you, Keyur. You are always welcome here," said Mina.

Jayesh and Keyur went back to the bedroom, did their homework, and started playing PlayStation. Keyur asked Jayesh, "With the funeral parlour downstairs, are people frightened to come to your house?"

"Yes," said Jayesh. "We don't get invited to a lot of our community functions, but we are used to it. My great-grandfather started the business in India. My grandfather used to help him. My grandfather inherited the funeral parlour in India, and my father used to help him in India. He basically did the odd jobs, what I am doing now. My grandfather had an opportunity to come to the UK, so he came and started this funeral parlour, which my dad helped him in, and the rest is history. That is how we got into the family business."

"That's interesting. I've always wondered why your dad opened a funeral parlour," said Keyur.

After Keyur went home, Jayesh was lying down on his bed when his mobile phone buzzed. He picked it up. It was his grandmother, Manorama, calling from India.

"Hello, Jayesh. How are you, my darling?" said Manorama.

"I'm fine, Dadi Ma, thanks. Is everything okay?" I said.

"I just wanted to talk to you about your gift, Jayesh," Manorama said. "When Geeta's spirit manifested in front of us, I want to explain to you why that happened, and so if it happens again, you won't get so frightened," she said.

"Sure, Dadi Maa, I said. "I was so frightened, I couldn't get to sleep for a few nights."

Manorama started to explain, "Jayesh, the older you get, the more your gift will get powerful."

"But I am just 13 years old," said Jayesh.

"In the spirit world, Jayesh, each day is like a year. So it's not about your actual age," she explained. "Different spirits have different, let's say, tricks up their sleeves. They can, if they want, manifest in front of you. Some spirits can even possess people as well. They can see into your soul. They will see you have a very pure soul, so you will have nothing to worry about. When Geeta manifested in our house, she couldn't do much—just talk loudly and have a small tantrum—that's all, because everyone in our house was pure-hearted."

"If you ever need to talk about anything, you can always call," Manorama said.

"Sure, I will. Thanks," I said.

"Goodbye, my love," Manorama said and put the phone down.

Manorama's phone call got Jayesh thinking, "Do I have to work at keeping my soul pure? Does it mean I can't lie or swear at my friends, or I can't swear when me and Keyur are playing football on the PlayStation? Because sometimes, a swear does come out of my mouth." Jayesh was a little worried. He didn't want a spirit to possess him or anyone in his family. He picked up his phone and called his grandmother again.

Manorama picked up on the first ring, "Hello, Jayesh, are you okay?"

"Yes," said Jayesh. "I just have a couple of questions for you."

"Sure, tell me, Jayesh, what's troubling you?"

Jayesh told his concerns to his grandmother. Manorama said, "Don't worry, Jayesh. Some people are not nice people. You are too young to understand. Some people talk behind people's back and don't like people who are doing well. And you get people who are so jealous and do evil things. You are too young to worry about that. Little white lies and swearing now and again is completely fine. Don't worry. You have fantastic parents who will guide you in your life."

"Thank you, Dadi Ma," Jayesh said.

Jayesh was relieved. He was so tired he fell asleep.

Chapter 9: International Spirits Part 1

The PlayStation screen glowed with a flicker of blue light, casting its blue shade on the wall. The shadows danced like specters, mocking our innocent banter as we lost ourselves in virtual glory. Keyur's laughter bounced off the wooden floorboards. "Haha, I am absolutely battering you today!" laughed Keyur. "Change your team to Arsenal, Jayesh. I told you Tottenham are rubbish," he said sarcastically. I was about to say something rude about his football team when just then a knock at the door startled me.

"Did you hear that?" "Hey," I said, mid-game, asking, the players frozen in the digital scene, the visual good enough to be more alive than the real.

Keyur shrugged, still gluing his eyes to the TV, his fingers flying fervently over the controller, missing the tension that had just filled the room. Lost in his gaming strategies, the sounds of virtual football drowning out reality, he was always good at blocking out the rest of the world.

There was another knock, and I shivered as it came, more insistent this time. Our playful competition was cut through. I gave a worried glance towards Keyur, when the door opened.

A soft movie was playing in the background, and my father, Prakash, paused it. He paused only briefly, then he got up from the couch, a sigh on his lips. He muttered to himself, more so than to anybody else, "Who could it be at this hour?" He moved toward the door, and there was no way to tell from his taut expression whether he was tired or not.

With the door opened, an unfamiliar face rose out of the evening shadows. His figure was silhouetted against the hallway light, looking like a ghost standing there waiting to be invited into the warmth of the home, waiting for the warmth. His features showed weariness, hope, and despair dancing in the depths of his eyes.

His voice was barely above a whisper as he apologised for the late intrusion. "My name is Raj. I've come from India to seek your help."

He shifted uncomfortably, and Prakash' face took on a careful mask of business-like demeanor. "Come in, please." He stepped slightly aside but allowed Raj into our sanctuary, albeit with a fractional hesitance. The door clicked shut; the warmth of the living space against cool evening air but decidedly chilly in its own way.

Raj took a further step in, leaning in to let our surroundings wash over him, flickering light of the television casting eerie shadows that wavered like ghosts on the walls. "I...I need to ask your help about my brother," he said, the load of his words weighed, practically.

"Brother?" Folding his arms across his chest, Prakash echoed. "What about him?"

I leaned forward, suddenly intrigued. I saw the gravity of the situation, and Raj's face twisted with sorrow. "He passed away unexpectedly." His voice cracked, unable to speak any further. "I suspect foul play."

My mother, Mina, walked into the living room, her being always soothed me as the scent of the parlor, which was filled with the smell of sandalwood incense. She noticed that she caught Raj's eye and gave a smile full of compassion, one that told him to keep going on. "I am so sorry for your loss," she said softly, wrapping herself around us like a comforting blanket. Mina said to Raj, "Please have a seat, let me get some nice masala tea. You must be tired after your long journey from India."

Keyur and Jayesh came into the living room. With every detail that came out of Raj's mouth, I felt the weight of his sorrow settle deeper into my chest. "Why do you think it was foul play?" said Prakash. "I am quite sure Arjun, my brother, was murdered," Prakash looked at Raj with a surprised look on his face.

I looked at Keyur; he had a concerned look on his eyebrows. My eyes met Raj's. He looked at me and said,

"Is your name Jayesh?" "Yes," I said. I could see the pain in his eyes. "I have read a lot about your special gifts."

"Can you contact him?" Raj asked, eyes pleading. "Because I've heard stories, I know, it sounds strange." Stories about your family. About... communication with the dead." Yet under it was an undertow of belief from which his voice trembled, afraid to relinquish his last hope.

My father shifted, considering the seriousness of their implications and the request. "We don't know if it's possible, but we can definitely try," he spoke after finally looking at me and then at Mina. "What do you think?" "Look Raj, my son does have a gift but he has only communicated with the spirits that are in my funeral parlour. You are from India, we haven't done this with international spirits."

I turned my head and looked at the floor as if it might have the answers to my thoughts. I remembered the memories of my grandmother telling me whispered tales of spirits and shadows that moved between worlds when I was younger. I was quite intrigued and wanted to see if I could be contacted by spirits from different countries.

Shivani, my little sister, had appeared at the edge of the room and broken the moment with youthful curiosity peeking through the seriousness. A teasing grin flitted across her face and she caught sight of me. "The ghostbuster begins to take form, Jayesh."

The air around us relaxed, allowing a second of levity in the very spirits of the bothering shadows that waited for us in the background. The spirit of an adventure kindled in me momentarily, but then the world of someone else's request crumbled down upon me.

I finally said, words tumbling from their places as I couldn't swallow them back, "We should try and contact Arjun." I felt that it was right, that it was a chance to help. "We can use his phone." Often, I would feel wanderlust... kind of as a feeling of excitement and dread about communicating with a spirit, but underneath that, I didn't know why, there was this force pushing me forward.

Raj said, "I have brought my brother's phone with me from India." Jayesh took Arjun's phone from Raj. Jayesh switched on the mobile phone. Jayesh could feel Raj looking at him intensely. Jayesh put the phone to his ear, but there was no sound, only static and crackling. "Hello," said Jayesh repeatedly. "Hello Arjun, are you there?"

"I'm sorry," I whispered and felt the disappointment come crashing down on the room, an extreme silence that magnified our fears.

Raj started slumping his shoulders in despair and put his brother's phone in his pocket. As soon as Raj put Arjun's phone in his pocket, the unexpected ringing of Arjun's phone startled us. Raj took the phone back out of his pocket. It echoed through the silence, and all eyes looked at him in shock.

"Go on," I said, my heart racing to match the curious urge.

Raj gave me the phone back, and when I took it, my palms were clammy against the cool of the device. Fear and determination entwined together, and I brought it to my ear.

"Hello?" My whisper was almost nonexistent, but I could feel the anticipation of what's to come ahead to find out the truth.

The mystery filled me with great excitement as I held the phone to my right ear, and the dead line burst into life with a crackle-laden voice. It was a voice that could not be described as anything other than vibrant, though it seemed to have been touched by death. I put down the glass and the unknown pressure of what I was about to unveil pushed into my throat, and I realized the presence of Arjun in death was as shocking as his life in life.

"Jayesh?" Pulling through the noise, just barely I heard it, or at least the name that came with it. It was a sensation or I could say a voice coming from the other side of the grave internationally. The atmosphere grew tense for a moment and I could actually see the air between us getting thicker with apprehension and fascination as a vice. "It is essential to share the incident with you. They took my life. I didn't see it coming."

I took a deep breath. I felt my heartbeat pounding in my head. "Arjun?" I said. His name was still strange sounding to my ears. My mother held my hand, which made the somber mood in the room a little bearable. "How can I help you, Arjun?"

He spoke with tears and trembling, progressing towards complete emotional breakdown in the emptiness he represented. "I was murdered, Jayesh. These he did without a second thought and at the worst possible moment, as far as my feelings were concerned."

There followed a silence, a heavy cloud, similar to that of a fog that enclosed us five. I looked at my father, now he looked really sad, his usual 'Iron Man' toughness had vanished. His face clouded with a deep intensity that it seemed his brows, which had crumbled with Arjun's words, were supporting his entire face.

"What do you mean, Arjun? You were murdered. Please tell us more, Arjun." I was trying to gather the information, desperately trying to find out the whole truth on what had happened to Arjun.

"They who I relied on... betrayed me. It is betrayal of the worst kind anyone could imagine." The severity of the tone Arjun used to say his next words made my stomach turn. "If all she wanted is money, all she needed to do is just ask. I would have given her everything. She was like a mother to me. Please help me, Jayesh. They have to know the truth for their own safety."

My fingers shook against the phone, and the cold structure comforted me amid the overwhelming feeling taking hold of me. This sobering of his plea bore considerable weight on me and squeezed the further understanding of the horror together into a criminal chest.

"Arjun, who is responsible for this?" My throat felt parched as the words seemed to lodge themselves in my throat, and I barely was able to utter them in a whisper.

"I... There is one thing I couldn't say," stuttering and the terror was clear in his voice. "They're always watching. But you need to dig deeper. You must connect the pieces." The words appeared to be a clue to the place in which he died.

Every word was said like daggers piercing through my heart; then the fear turned into a fiery resolve. I pictured the events in graphic detail as if I really could see him die, and in the same darkness being betrayed.

With every word Arjun was saying to Jayesh, you could see the anticipation in Raj's face to find out what his brother was telling him. Raj was shaking nervously in the corner, a combination of hope and disbelief emanating from him.

"I have to," I said out loud, although it wasn't necessary. I said it more to myself. The drive to help arose in me and was burning brightly as if it was the only light in the advancing darkness. Arjun deserved justice, a voice after his life had been so valued and taken away.

Prakash went quiet for a while to grasp the immense confusion happening around him. His shoulders looked like a huge burden rested on him, to guess that family is inextricably linked not only with love but with the secrets that are hidden deep inside.

"Please let me know more, Arjun," I repeated. "Arjun, please tell me everything. I need all the information so we can help you. Please don't hold back; we need to know everything."

"Jayesh, my family is very close to each other. I have two brothers. My oldest brother is Vijay who is 60 years old and my younger brother is called Raj who is 52 years old. My brother Vijay's wife is my bhabi. Bhabi is what you call your older brother's wife by respect. I had been diagnosed with cancer and was having treatment. While I was having treatment I was getting quite emotional. I think it might have been the side effects of my treatment. I thought to myself I should have a will made. So I told my brothers and my sister-in-law. They said don't be silly, you are going to be OK. My brother had a lovely restaurant in Mumbai but business was suffering after the COVID lockdowns and the increase in prices on utilities and stock. In my will I gave my 3 houses to my older brother Vijay. I had 2 apartments which I left Raj and I split my shares I had in a diamond mine with Vijay and Raj."

Mina had to take my hand, which she grasped ferociously in a bid to force courage into me. Jayesh looked more and more emotional. "Don't worry," Jayesh said to his mother, "we will help him," she said soothingly, the sentiment in her voice was all motherly. In her eyes, there was the determination to make something out of hatred, to stand for the invaluable lessons and true bond that your family provides even in the worst of situations.

"It sounds like Arjun has been really hurt," said Keyur. "We need to help him," said Jayesh, looking at his mum and dad.

Finally, Prakash just nodded his head in agreement, and there was a clear understanding that existed between us. "All right," he replied at last, his voice quite authoritative but with the slightest hint of tension. This status implies that individuals working in such an environment should exercise care and try to amass whatever they can. "We owe it to Arjun."

The form that was beside me was steady, if not anchored itself, though I squeezed Mina's hand once again. "A storm is coming," Jayesh said solemnly, meeting everyone's eyes. "We will face this together, Jayesh."

"Arjun, what happened? Please tell me so I can tell Raj, who is next to me, how you were murdered."

Arjun gets very emotional and says, "Is Raj next to you?"

"Yes," I say.

"Please tell him they all have to be careful of Urvashi bhabi," Arjun says.

"One weekend Vijay and Raj go to Surat, which is a town in Gujarat, to our elderly uncle to see how he is.

Urvashi bhabi was getting very friendly, I found after I had done the will.

When Raj and Vijay went for the weekend to Surat, that evening bhabi phoned me to come for dinner.

She said, 'I am making your favourite minced lamb with potatoes and hot chapatis and basmati rice.'

I said, 'Fantastic, I will be there at around 7 pm.'

I was about to leave when bhabi phoned again.

She said, 'Arjun please don't leave because I have an emergency at your brother's restaurant so I need to go to the restaurant.'

I said, 'Do you need me to come to the restaurant to give you a hand?'

She said, 'No, don't worry, it's nothing serious.'

Urvashi bhabi said, 'Vikas, my nephew, is on his way to my house to give the food to me.'"

"When I got the food from my nephew Vikas, I was so happy.

I was so hungry I put the food on my dining table.

Got my plate and a bottle of beer.

I put on the football on the television.

The minced lamb was so tasty but after a few bites I started to feel hot and sweaty.

I started to feel dizzy and was finding it hard to breathe.

I collapsed on the floor clutching my chest.

I couldn't speak or move.

Then my eyes closed and all of a sudden I could see myself hovering above my body."

As it sunk in that our new mission involved entering a coming darkness, I took a deep breath and realized it was a chilling activity that would involve a confrontation of evil, not only from the outside world but the evil that was falling within our society.

That very moment marked the decision-making moment.

We would seek justice, not just for Arjun but for every whispered ghost that begs to be heard.

Chapter 9: Uncovering the Murder (Part 2)

We could all see that Arjun had been really hurt. Raj couldn't believe what he was hearing.

"I died in the hands of my bhabi Urvashi, my older brother's wife, a murderer. I always knew she was materialistic and jealous, but who would think she was capable of murder?" You could hear the heartbreak in Arjun's voice. You could sense he was crying.

Raj went pale. "I can't believe it," said Raj. "I always thought we were a close family, but my brother's wife was always the one causing fights. She always fought with my mother when she was alive about why she had less jewellery than her friend, and when she had to cook for the family, she would always make a big fuss."

Raj explained to my mum and dad that when older brother Vijay got married, we all used to live in one big house, but when my Urvashi bhabi came to live with us, there were always small arguments and a lot of animosity in the house.

"So when my mother passed away, me and Raj decided to move out so my brother Vijay could have a peaceful life with his wife and son. My brother Vijay was so upset when me and Raj moved out, but we all knew Urvashi bhabi didn't want us around."

Arjun said, "I still can't believe what she did. I would never have guessed, even in my wildest imagination, that when I had my last dinner, my favourite minced lamb with potatoes would be my last ever meal."

I could see the tears stream down Raj's face. I imagined that moment and the moment of his death, which I envisioned as a cloak of eerie simplicity. Cold sweat prickled down my back.

I whispered "Arjun" through the knot of urgency choking my voice. "Raj has been right next to me," I said to Arjun.

"Really!!!" Arjun's tone slowly went from anguish to pure explosion. "Please put him on the line."

Raj's brow knitted with excitement as I glanced over my shoulder, and his excitement made my pulse quicken.

"Um... but," I muttered hesitantly, "I can't, Arjun," I said. "Only I can hear you. I have been repeating word by word everything you have been telling me."

"What do you mean? Why can't I speak to him?" said Arjun angrily.

"Only I have the gift to communicate with you, Arjun. If I put Raj on the phone, you won't be able to hear him, and he will only be able to hear static and crackling."

"Jayesh, you need to tell Raj to get the police to investigate what I have told you. First of all, Raj has to get the police to get an autopsy done on my body so they will know the cause of death is poisoning.

He has to tell the police there is evidence of Urvashi bhabi poisoning me.

Tell Raj to tell the police to find Mukesh's pharmacy; it's in Pune near the multiplex cinema.

Tell them to check the CCTV footage, it shows Urvashi bhabi's face clearly purchasing the poison, and they will be able to get receipts from the pharmacy as well, please."

Raj looked at my mum and dad and said, "Why would she do this?"

"Greed," said my dad straight away. "Money makes people do evil things.

This is not the first and it won't be the last case that people do crazy things for money," said Prakash.

Raj wanted to say something, but he didn't know how to say it.

"What is it?" said my mum.

"Can I ask a question to Arjun, please, Jayesh?"

"Sure, tell me," I said.

"Please ask Arjun: did Vijay, my brother, have anything to do with this?"

I asked Arjun the question Raj wanted me to ask.

Arjun said immediately, "No, not at all. No one else had anything to do with this."

You could see the sense of relief on Raj's face.

"I had to ask," said Raj.

I felt the burden of empathy and a cold sense of dread wrap itself over my shoulders like a shroud as I processed all that was swirling in my mind.

Arjun's influence still cast itself between us, his hurry running through our souls, as if we both were fully alive to the dark labyrinth in front of us, full of deception, grief, and anger.

My dad said, "Raj, you need to call India quickly. They need to start this investigation immediately."

"Yes, you are right," said Raj.

Raj dialled the police in India.

I watched him, watching the pained expression across his face of anger, grief, and determination.

The phone was almost pressed to his ear as he started to recount the accusations.

His hands were trembling, shaking with disbelief and fury.

"Hello?" He spoke with urgency.

"Yes, yes, this is Raj Patel calling from abroad."

I held my breath, trying to hear the slightest sound of what was taking place on the other side of the line.

It was the sense of urgency, thick with history, that surrounded his family.

"Listen," he said in a harsh voice.

Raj told them who he was and all his personal information that the police needed to verify who he was.

Then Raj began to tell them everything.

"My brother Arjun, he was murdered.

I have reasons to believe, and I have proof, that my sister-in-law Urvashi has murdered my brother Arjun.

I need you to perform an autopsy on his body because he has poison in his body which killed him.

I have all the proof you need.

Please begin with the autopsy.

I will get on the next flight from London and see you at the police station tomorrow."

The words dripped with gravity, going deeper into our world, into our shared reality, into the heartbreak happening in the living room, silence everywhere.

It was hard to digest this sudden shift around us, the urgency that infused its very way into Raj's words while he waded in and out of grief, anger, and love of Arjun.

"This needs to be investigated.

My sister-in-law Urvashi purchased the poison she murdered me with.

You need to check Mukesh's Pharmacy, that's where she bought the poison in Pune.

It's next to the multiplex cinema.

If you face any issue, it will be in the CCTV footage!

You can see her face clearly in the footage!

Look, I will be there tomorrow.

I will go through it in person with you.

But please get the autopsy done immediately."

Tension oozed from him; a palpable desperation seemed to be firing the air.

Both Prakash and Mina glanced at each other worriedly, their faces showing concern swirling around them faster than it could revert.

I felt their pain, their unbreakable need to safeguard their family from the violent storm of betrayal.

I could sense Raj turn back to us, lighting a soft pleading in the warmth of his gaze.

Raj ended the call to the police with a request for urgent action.

There was great contrast between his fierce determination and the stark chill creeping through the room, as though the weight of the world was anchored to the ground in front of him.

Raj put the phone down and turned to face us.

He said, "Thank you so much, everyone.

I don't know how I will ever repay your kindness and the help you have given me."

Raj gave Jayesh a big hug and said, "Whenever you are all in India, please come and see me.

I need to leave now.

I have to catch the next flight back to Mumbai."

Mina started to step forward.

"Raj," she said softly, "just... take care of yourself."

Her concern formed a tender picture over the bleakness that tightened before us.

Raj tried to project calmness as he replied, "Of course I will, Mina bhen, thank you."

Grief and resolve tangled in his expression as he got in the Uber cab he had called, leaving us behind.

The next few days were quite surreal.

Life went on as normal.

I went to school.

Keyur came home some evenings to play on the PlayStation.

Shivani was making things with her bead sets.

Mum was helping dad with paperwork from his funeral parlour, and dad was always busy in the funeral parlour with his staff.

One evening we were all having dinner while watching the Indian news channel.

Mum and dad loved to put that on the TV to keep up with what was going on in their home country, when we saw a reporter interviewing Raj and his brother Vijay.

The reporter was saying, "How did you know your brother was murdered?"

Raj said, "I just had a feeling.

My brother was very fit and healthy, so how could someone like that die all of a sudden?

So I told the police to investigate his death.

They had an autopsy done of my brother and found he was poisoned."

Vijay said, "The police did a thorough investigation, and they found out that my wife had poisoned my brother."

The next clip showed the police taking Vijay's wife into custody, handcuffed and put in a police car.

Raj told the reporter, "Thank you to the police for doing a fantastic job," and Raj gave a wink and smile to the camera.

"Well, that is fantastic news," said Prakash.

"And you can see he gave that wink and smile to you, Jayesh," said Mina.

"Dad," I said, "now do you think we can help more spirits and people from different countries?"

"Well, let's see, Jayesh.

Let's see."

* 9 7 8 1 9 6 5 8 7 5 4 6 9 *